Breathing filled her ear.

Not the creepy heavy kind like in a horror movie, but disturbing all the same. The person wanted her to know he was on the line. But to what end?

"I know you're there."

"Hello, Detective Bowman."

The hairs stood on the back of her neck. "What do you want?"

"You. Your time is coming to an end." The whispered words sent the sensation of icy fingers creeping up her spine and onto her scalp.

Her mind spun to last night. Bits of memory flashed like short video clips. Sitting in her chair. Taking the sleeping medication. Hearing a noise. The shadowy figure. The pain in her head. The smell of smoke. The words *sweet dreams*.

She jolted upright and slammed the phone down.

Someone had done this to her, and he knew where to find her.

"What's wrong?"

Cassidy jerked her gaze to Kyle, who stood in the doorway. "He tried to kill me."

Two-time Genesis Award-winner **Sami A. Abrams** and her husband live in Northern California, but she'll always be a Kansas girl at heart. She enjoys visiting her two grown children and spoiling their sweet fur babies. Most evenings, if Sami's not watching sports, you'll find her engrossed in a romantic suspense novel. She thinks a crime plus a little romance is the recipe for a great story. Visit her at www.samiaabrams.com.

Books by Sami A. Abrams

Love Inspired Suspense

Deputies of Anderson County

Buried Cold Case Secrets
Twin Murder Mix-Up
Detecting Secrets
Killer Christmas Evidence

Visit the Author Profile page at LoveInspired.com.

KILLER
CHRISTMAS
EVIDENCE

SAMI A. ABRAMS

LOVE INSPIRED SUSPENSE
INSPIRATIONAL ROMANCE

LOVE INSPIRED® SUSPENSE
INSPIRATIONAL ROMANCE

Recycling programs for this product may not exist in your area.

ISBN-13: 978-1-335-59771-7

Killer Christmas Evidence

Copyright © 2023 by Sherryl Abramson

For questions and comments about the quality of this book, please contact us at CustomerService@Harlequin.com.

Love Inspired
22 Adelaide St. West, 41st Floor
Toronto, Ontario M5H 4E3, Canada
www.LoveInspired.com

Printed in U.S.A.

And we know that all things work together for good to them that love God, to them who are the called according to his purpose.
—*Romans* 8:28

This book is dedicated to my Crime Scene Crew. You ladies are awesome! Thank you so much for joining me on this journey and helping me tell the world about my books.

ONE

The police report burned in Detective Cassidy Bowman's hand. Accidental death due to drunk driving. No way. She knew her cousin better than that.

Laura didn't drink, and neither did Cassidy after a close friend from high school died in a drunk driving accident. Cassidy didn't care that the lab had found alcohol in Laura's bloodstream and an empty bottle in her car. The report had it wrong.

Cassidy intended to find evidence to support that fact—one of the reasons she'd temporarily moved to Valley Springs, thirty miles from her home in Brentwood, Indiana. The second reason? Killings throughout the surrounding counties that her boss refused to recognize as the result of a serial killer on the loose.

"Talk to me, Laura. What really happened to you?" Cassidy sank deeper into the brown overstuffed leather recliner provided by her rental apartment. Twisting a strand of her hair, she flipped the page and continued to read. The end table lamp beside her illuminated the papers. And the blazing fire in the fireplace on the far wall added to the glow in the room. A cozy atmosphere, if not for the confusing conclusions in the document.

A witness to her cousin's accident had her scratching

her head. Cassidy studied the statement. What bothered her about it?

She tapped her phone. "Remind me to reinterview the man who saw Laura's accident and witnessed someone helping her." After setting a reminder for the morning, she returned the device to her pocket.

Her attention drifted to the twinkling multicolored lights on the Christmas tree in the corner of the room. The crackling fire added warmth to the cold evening, and the scent of burning wood comforted her.

Christmas was coming, and she had no desire to celebrate, but the pine smell of the tree and sparkling lights had lifted the weight of depression—at least a little. The past year she'd spiraled toward a dark abyss, and she struggled not to let it take her under.

Her landlord, Mr. Webster, had gone all out on decorations at the main house and guilted her into a tree for the front window of the garage-turned-apartment. Saying no—not an option.

The older man had taken her in and made her feel special. More than her father had ever done. Colonel Trevor Bowman treated her like a soldier and not a young girl who'd lost her mother to cancer. Cassidy had never felt like enough, constantly striving and falling short. Others thought of her as driven. Ha! More like self-preservation in her father's world of perfection.

Until this year, Cassidy had always seen Christmas as a time for hope, thanks to Meredith, the older neighbor lady who'd taken her to church and helped her through her teenage years. Well, too bad Cassidy didn't have hope anymore. Being alone in the world did that to a person.

But she'd had that pity party earlier, and it hadn't gotten her anywhere, so she pushed the loneliness aside and concentrated on the investigation. Her father had demanded excellence and hadn't allowed emotions to interfere. He'd died years ago but left his mark on her life.

She tucked her black-and-red-plaid pajama–clad legs under her, wrapped her hand around the mug of hot tea and perused the document for the second time. She'd switched from coffee to decaffeinated tea weeks ago, hoping not to use the sleeping pills that sat next to her on the small square table. She'd only had mild success, but with the way her evening had gone, she hadn't held out hope of avoiding the prescription.

Laying the copy of Laura's file neatly aside, she picked up another. She'd scoured the surrounding areas for unsolved suspicious deaths and accidents where family members had protested the results of the investigation. Because in her mind, that's what Laura's death was—murder. She was confident that someone had killed her cousin and made it look like an accident. Cassidy wanted to find the person responsible and clear Laura's name.

When her boss at Brentwood PD discovered her using police department resources for her personal hunt for the truth, he gave her a sympathetic look, then told her to take time off and not come back until she'd worked out her issues.

Issues? Of course she had issues. Her best friend and partner, Amber Lofton, died during a drug raid Cassidy had commanded. Then three months later, her cousin's life ended in a tragic accident, leaving her alone in the world. Two deaths that never should have happened.

She lifted her hand and made a fist. The burn scars that wrapped around her lower arm and the top of her hand stretched and turned white. She'd paid a physical price during the raid when the door exploded seconds before they'd planned to breach the house, but the emotional scars had dug in deeper.

When she'd regained consciousness after the explosion, her team lay across the lawn, and someone used a jacket to slap out the flames that threatened to burn more than her arm.

She'd suffered severe second-degree burns, a concussion and lacerations over her back and legs from flying debris. The hospital stay had felt like an eternity, but at least she'd lived. Unlike Amber.

The claws of guilt raked across her heart. Why hadn't it been her instead of her best friend? Survivor's guilt. That's what the therapist had called it. She called it her mistake. If only she'd read the situation faster...

The walk down memory lane left her wallowing in self-pity. Someday the loss wouldn't hurt so badly. She hoped. Until then, she'd work on finding justice for her cousin and prove her worth as a detective. Failure hadn't sat well. Replaying the tactical plan and mentally sorting through the intel hadn't given her a different outcome. It shouldn't have happened. But she'd missed something, and that was on her.

The new file angled toward the lamp, Cassidy settled deeper into her chair, refusing to give way to the pit of depression that threatened to swallow her whole.

A soft snick came from her right.

Cassidy resisted the urge to grab her gun off the coffee table and froze. She tilted her head and listened.

Nothing.

Great. Now her mind had decided to play tricks on her. Her pulse rate settled.

She flipped open the file on Bradford Technology CEO Tim Raines. Two shots to the chest during an in-home burglary. His wife, adamant she'd set the security alarm. Cassidy's finger trailed the list of stolen items. A few pieces of jewelry and inexpensive electronics. That didn't make sense. A house filled with high-priced belongings, and the attacker takes minor things? She continued to read and halted at the words "Peeping Tom multiple nights prior to the crime." The basics fit her theory, especially the prowler, but the location was the key.

Cassidy checked the address and closed her eyes, visualizing the site. It fit. The crime was one of *his*. She leaned her head back on the cushion, letting the information settle in her brain. Her serial killer moved to new hunting grounds after a few kills so the police wouldn't link the crimes.

The guy tended to concentrate on the wealthy in power positions. Beyond that, his victims varied in gender and age. And then there were people, like her cousin, who didn't fit at all. But Cassidy knew in her gut that Laura's accident had a connection to the other crimes. She'd never dealt with this kind of killer before. Cassidy knew he'd taken the life of at least thirteen people. But how did she prove her theory?

Exhaustion flooded her system. Her eyes drooped. She debated calling it a night. But if she headed to bed, sleep would refuse to come. And she desperately needed it. She closed the file and added it to the pile.

What choice did she have? Medication, her only answer for rest tonight. She glanced over and spotted the bottle of prescription sleeping pills. Giving in to reality, she dropped one tablet onto her palm and sighed. So much for avoiding the chemical help. She popped the pill into her mouth and swallowed.

When would insomnia cease and her life return to normal? She missed her job and her coworkers. More than anything, she missed the peace in her life. She and God had been close once, but after the year she'd had, He seemed far away.

A clunk came from the kitchen.

That was not her imagination. Someone *was* in her apartment.

She'd rented the garage apartment from the lovely Mr. Webster, an elderly man who lived in the main house. Maybe her landlord had let himself in. As soon as the idea came, it left. Mr. Webster never entered without knocking. He'd promised her privacy, and so far, he'd kept his word.

No. It couldn't be him.

She hurried to unfold her legs and reached for her SIG-Sauer on the coffee table where she'd placed it hours ago after coming home from the tiny office that she'd rented to keep her investigations private.

Why hadn't she trusted her gut instinct about the earlier sound?

A blow to the back of her head sent her sprawling. Her weapon clattered across the wood floor, and white lights streaked across her vision. She lifted her blurry gaze to a figure standing over her.

The shadows and the haze from her head wound refused to give away her attacker's features. Her eyes closed of their own accord, and she drifted on a dreamlike state.

Hands clutched her wrists. Her assailant pulled her arms above her head and tugged. Her body slid on the floor, the movement making her shoulder muscles burn.

The man released his grip, and her head bounced on a hard surface, sending pain slicing through her. The pounding inside her head increased. She struggled to put the pieces of what happened together.

Heat warmed her, and the rough surface beneath signaled her brain that she lay on the brick next to the fireplace. But her mind wouldn't function beyond that basic awareness, and her body seemed worthless to fight back.

Glass shattered beside her, and the scent of alcohol burned her nose.

The harder she tried, the less clarity she achieved.

Smoke invaded her senses. Pops and crackles sounded next to her. Fear swirled within, but her body refused to move. The heat crawled closer, sending panic climbing up her throat. She couldn't endure the pain from burns again. She just couldn't. *God, where are You?*

Cassidy fought to open her eyes—to get away. But her lids remained closed.

Hot breath flicked across her cheek, and a whisper met her ear. "Sweet dreams."

She struggled to respond, but the weight of her head and limbs proved it impossible.

The serial killer she'd stumbled upon had targeted her as his next victim. It was the only thing that made sense.

The burning scent of pine and smoke clogged her throat. She gasped for air. A blanket of darkness fell over her and took her under.

I'm sorry, Laura. Your killer will continue to go free.

Detective Kyle Howard's gaze traveled around Dennis and Charlotte's home.

The Christmas tree branches drooped under the weight of the overabundance of ornaments. Garland draped from one window to the next, and decorations filled every corner and flat surface available. It looked like Christmas had thrown up in every room of the house.

No doubt the couple wanted a memorable holiday for their five-year-old girls whom they had met for the first time several months ago. Dennis became a sudden single dad when a social worker had dropped off his daughter, whom he knew nothing about. And Charlotte discovered that her baby hadn't died, but was a victim of an illegal adoption ring.

Kyle appreciated the efforts for his honorary nieces,

but the stark reminder of the loss of his fiancée, Amber, made his heart ache.

Music played in the background, and Kyle's friends and coworkers chatted while the little girls and their two dogs bounced around, making everyone laugh. Keith and Amy's little boy, Connor, toddled from one person to another, soaking up the love in the room.

And then there was Melanie. Kyle glanced at his coworker and friend Jason, who had his arms wrapped around his wife and his hands splayed on her nine-month-pregnant belly. The baby, Jason and Melanie's first, made child number four in their tight work family.

He'd hoped to add to the growing group of little ones, but his dream had evaporated with Amber's death.

He adored his extended family of friends, but nine months and the first Christmas without Amber left a hole in his life. All he'd ever wanted was what his grandparents had had—a long, strong marriage to someone he considered his best friend. He'd found that match, but his happily ever after ended before it had started.

Except for his partner, Doug, who had his wife ripped away from him, his team had found their helpmates in life, and he should be part of that group—but wasn't.

God, it hurts so bad.

Joy was beyond his ability tonight, and he couldn't fake the cheer anymore. Kyle tossed his dessert plate in the garbage and made his rounds with a quick goodbye to his friends.

He hoped to escape before his boss zeroed in on him, but Dennis stopped him on the front porch.

"The ducking out is noticed." Sheriff Dennis Monroe, his boss and friend, stood blocking his path.

Kyle sighed. So much for a clean getaway.

"I'm not going to push." Dennis rested his hand on

Kyle's shoulder. "Call if you need a listening ear. You know I'm here for you."

He knew. Dennis had helped him those first few weeks when Kyle thought he'd never survive the heartache.

A smile tried to curve on the corner of his mouth but failed. He had a great boss and appreciated the man's offer. But right now, he wanted to grieve in private.

"Thanks." He swallowed the growing lump in his throat. "I'll see you tomorrow." Kyle ducked around his boss and headed to his truck.

He maneuvered through Valley Springs, heading home alone, wishing, not for the first time tonight, that he had Amber beside him celebrating her favorite holiday. She loved Christmas and would've enjoyed the evening with his friends.

Tears stung his eyes. He blinked away the moisture.

Kyle took the long way home, hoping the Christmas lights would boost his spirits. He wove through the streets known for colorful displays.

He actually smiled as he approached Mr. Webster's house. Kyle slowed to enjoy the sight. Multicolored lights twinkled under the night sky. A handcrafted wooden nativity scene stood prominent in the front yard. The man had outdone himself this year.

Kyle made a mental note to bring his "nieces and nephew" to see the decorations.

As he eased by the house, smoke swirled from the older man's garage apartment. Kyle stopped, shifted into reverse and took a second look. Flames flickered in the front window.

What in the world?

Mr. Webster rushed down the front steps of the main house in a robe and slippers, frantically waving his hands.

Kyle slammed his truck into Park and jumped from the vehicle.

"She's inside!" Mr. Webster pointed to the apartment.

"Who?" As if it mattered, but Kyle wanted to know what name to call out. He hadn't met the current tenant.

"Cassie."

"Call 911."

"Already done." The older man put his hands on his knees to catch his breath.

Kyle sprinted to the entrance and tried the knob. Locked. He pounded on the door. "Cassie! Open up!" When no one answered, Kyle raised his boot and struck the door. The wood splintered but didn't break. On the second kick, the frame fractured, and the door flew open.

A wave of smoke rolled out from the apartment. He moved to the side and lifted his arm in a lame attempt to block the black haze.

Lifting the neckline of his sweater over his nose and mouth, he let his gaze roam the room. He spotted a body lying near the fireplace not far from the Christmas tree that glowed with flames.

He grabbed a small blanket that lay over the back of the couch and slapped at the fire that crept toward the woman.

The flames persisted and crawled closer. A dark gray cloud of smoke hung from the ceiling. The foul air clogged his throat and stung his eyes. He had to hurry. The fire hadn't stretched far, but the smoke could kill, and promised to do so if he didn't act fast.

Kyle increased the tempo of his assault to snuff out the fire.

Sweat beaded on his forehead and trickled down his back. His attempts had slowed the spread, but the threat continued to take hold. He refused to allow the woman to die on his watch. He had to get to her before it was too late.

After what felt like an hour but had only taken less than a minute, he'd cleared a path to the woman. Without delay, he lifted the lady into his arms and hurried from the apartment.

The cold December air, a jolt from the heat of the fire, sent chills zipping down his back, freezing the sweat droplets on his skin. Fresh air entered his lungs, clearing the smoke he'd inhaled.

He'd made it out of the blaze and now had a newfound admiration for the three men from the Bible who'd endured the fiery furnace.

Sirens wailed in the distance, sending relief through his system for the first time since he'd spotted the blaze.

"Here." Mr. Webster motioned to the front porch of his home, where he'd laid out a blanket away from the cold, wet ground.

It had snowed recently, and even though the temperatures had melted most of it away, a thin layer of ice lingered on the dead grass.

His boots crunched across the lawn. He carefully maneuvered the steps with his precious cargo. "Thanks." Kyle laid the woman down.

Mr. Webster handed him a first-aid kit and pulled a patio chair close. "Cassie, honey. Wake up."

The woman moaned, but her eyes remained closed.

Kyle checked her pulse and breathing and found no immediate danger. He shed his jacket, covered her torso to help keep her warm, and brushed the hair from her face. He wiped away the soot with his shirtsleeve and got his first good look at the person he'd rescued.

"Cassidy?" No, please, not her.

Lord, not now. Not at Christmas. I'm struggling enough without having to face the person whose actions killed Amber.

"I take it you've met."

"Oh yeah, we've met." Boy had they, but he'd keep the truth to himself for now.

Mr. Webster clutched Cassidy's hand and held it. "She's such a sweet girl."

Kyle huffed. Sweet. Not the word he'd use to describe her. At least not anymore.

A small porch light glowed above, and for the first time since getting her out of the apartment, he noticed blood on the blanket near the back of her head.

His first-responder training took over. He retrieved the medical gloves from the first-aid kit and slipped one on. With a gentle touch, he slid his fingers over the area. He lifted his hand. Blood streaked the blue glove. "She's got a nice gash here."

"What do you need?"

The fire truck's red lights filled the air, and the siren whined one last time and went silent. Kyle pointed to the paramedics. "They just arrived." He pulled the glove off inside out and tossed it aside.

His firefighter friends dropped from the truck and unrolled the hoses. He didn't envy their job. Tonight had more than confirmed he'd made the correct choice not pursuing a career in firefighting. He'd take law enforcement any day over facing a fire.

Rachel and Peter, the paramedics on duty, made their way to the front porch.

Peter set down his duffel. "What do we have?"

"Thirty-year-old female. Cassidy Bowman. A Brentwood PD detective." The smoke had given him a gruff, deeper tone.

Mr. Webster raised a bushy white eyebrow.

Kyle chose to ignore him and continued. "She has a laceration on the back of her head and with the smoke, most likely a case of smoke inhalation."

"Sounds like you have some too." Peter offered him oxygen.

Kyle considered refusing but decided against it. "Maybe a little. Thanks." He accepted the mask and sucked in the clean air. His eyes closed at the relief. He scooted over to give the paramedics room to work on Cassidy.

Rachel placed an oxygen mask over Cassidy's nose and mouth and pushed the sleeve of her pajama top up her arm to take her blood pressure. "Whoa," she said as she inspected the burn scars. "These aren't very old. What happened?"

Kyle swallowed hard at the devastating results of that case. He'd known she'd suffered burns, but seeing the severity shocked him. "A drug raid gone bad. Cassidy got caught in the effects of an explosion."

"Well, that would do it." Rachel took Cassidy's blood pressure and pulse. "All seems normal."

Within minutes, the fire was out, and Captain Phillips strode their way with a scowl on his face.

"Captain." Kyle stood and shook the man's hand.

"Detective Howard."

"What's the assessment?" He wondered if the tree had dried out and caused the fire. A common occurrence when people ignored the watering instructions for real trees.

"You know we have to take a look when it cools down."

Kyle waited the man out. The fire captain had a habit of protesting then giving his opinion.

Phillips pursed his lips and shook his head. "Initial look, the tree was the origin of the fire. Unsure what started it. I'm assuming you found the lady by the fireplace."

"I did."

"We found a broken wine bottle on the brick, and one of my guys grabbed these off the end table." Phillips handed him a bottle of prescription medicine.

Kyle read the description. His head jerked up. "Antidepressants?"

Rachel leaned over his shoulder, grabbed his hand and twisted to read the label. "Could be a sleeping aid. These work for both."

Captain Phillips crossed his arms. "Either way, they don't mix with alcohol."

Kyle shook his head in disbelief. "The meds, I can understand. But the alcohol? Not her style."

"How well do you know her?" Peter asked.

"Well enough to know that she doesn't drink." Kyle remembered the story about her best friend's car accident. In all the time he'd spent at Amber and Cassidy's place, he'd never seen her drink. Even after she'd worked a horrific accident with multiple fatalities.

He'd joined Amber and her team, including Cassidy, at a bar that evening. Most of the officers drank to kill the images burned into their brains. But like Amber, Cassidy hadn't touched the stuff. One of the reasons she and Amber had roomed well together. Neither partied and both agreed to keep the apartment alcohol free.

Phillips pointed to Cassidy's arm. "Maybe those scars changed things."

Kyle scratched the stubble on his jaw. "It's possible, I guess." What did he really know about her now? Nothing. Because he'd walked away and never intended to see her again.

"When was the last time the two of you talked?"

"Nine months ago."

Captain Phillips stared at him, but Kyle refused to go into details.

Cassidy groaned, and her eyes fluttered open. Her lack of focus concerned him.

"Hi there. I'm Rachel." The paramedic leaned over Cassidy. "How are you feeling?"

"Been better."

Kyle cringed at Cassidy's raspy voice. The smoke had done damage before he'd pulled her out.

"Do you remember what happened?" Rachel continued her questions.

She shook her head and winced.

Rachel patted her shoulder. "Try to stay still."

Cassidy lifted a hand to her forehead. "Yeah, I figured that out." Her gaze shifted to the surroundings. "Where am I?"

"Mr. Webster's porch." Kyle studied her reaction, wondering if the meds and alcohol had made her memory fuzzy. Or had the head wound caused the issue?

Cassidy closed her eyes long enough that he thought she'd fallen asleep. When she opened them, worry flickered behind her gaze. "Better question. Who am I?"

He glanced at Peter then back to Cassidy. "Wait. You don't know?"

Terrified eyes stared back at him. "No."

So much for walking away from his painful past. Amber would clock him for not helping her best friend. He had to stay until he made sure Cassidy would recover.

Kyle inhaled. "Take it easy. We'll figure it out."

What was Cassidy doing in Valley Springs?

Kyle paced the waiting room at Valley Springs General Hospital. The light green walls closed in on him. He'd never wanted to see Cassidy Bowman ever again. The woman had failed his fiancée, then hadn't contacted him and explained what happened.

A tinge of guilt poked at him. Maybe when Amber died, he'd ignored Cassidy and blamed her for failing his fiancée, then changed his phone number. Okay, so that was on him. But Cassidy was, after all, the task force commander, and the people under her command were her responsibility. And she'd botched her duty.

He ran a hand through his hair. The shock of seeing her had worn off, but the hurt lingered.

Kyle had called his boss, and Sheriff Monroe had told him to stay with Cassidy while he did a little digging into why a Brentwood Police Department detective, a town thirty miles away, was in Valley Springs, Indiana.

All Kyle wanted to do was go home and crawl under the covers and forget the holidays. He'd promised himself to stay until the doctor confirmed Cassidy had minor injuries. But no, Dennis had stuck him babysitting her until they released her from the hospital. Professional courtesy and all that. Kyle huffed. Why him? Keith had a much better bedside manner.

Kyle rubbed his gritty eyes with his finger and thumb. What a way to have your past thrown in your face.

Boots struck the hard floor, pulling him from his grumbling. He turned and spotted his boss striding down the hall.

"Dennis." He shook the man's hand.

"Hey, Kyle. Are you doing okay?" The sheriff squinted, doing a visual assessment.

"My eyes itch, and I'm still coughing, but overall, I'm good." As if Kyle's body wanted to prove a point, his lungs protested and sent him into a coughing fit.

"Are you sure about that?" Dennis raised a brow, but Kyle waved him off. "Any word on Cassidy?"

"No. Doc came in about two hours ago after they admitted her and told me he'd let me know when I could talk with her. He hasn't been back since."

Dennis motioned toward the chairs. "Have a seat. Let's chat."

That didn't sound good, but Kyle followed his boss into

the waiting room and collapsed onto the cushioned chair. "What's up?"

Dennis joined him, unzipped his coat and removed his black stocking cap. "I spoke with Cassidy's supervisor."

"And?"

"She's on forced leave." Dennis ran a hand over the back of his neck. "He's worried about her mental state. He told me she's obsessed with her cousin Laura's death."

"The car accident VSPD investigated six months ago?" Kyle had heard about the accident and had asked to read the report. It stated a drunk driving incident. He'd questioned the findings himself due to Cassidy and Laura's pact not to touch alcohol after their friend's death. But things changed, so he'd let his concern go, especially after reading the autopsy report, indicating a high blood alcohol level.

"The same. Cassidy believes her cousin was murdered and that there's a serial killer out there wreaking havoc on the citizens of Indiana."

The news jolted him. He'd known Cassidy a long time and had never seen her overreact. In fact, quite the opposite. Her meticulous behavior and thoroughness was one of the reasons the failed raid confused him. "Is there any truth to it?"

"Not that her captain believes." Dennis fidgeted with his hat. "I know it's a sore subject and brings back a lot of bad memories, but I could use your insight."

Kyle wanted to spout off about Cassidy's carelessness and that she didn't deserve any accolades from him. But the truth was the truth. "She's not the type to grasp at things that aren't there. Amber spoke highly of her investigative skills. Cassidy's nothing but logical. In fact, she's a bit obsessive-compulsive."

"So, this is out of character for her?"

"Seeing a serial killer that the captain believes doesn't exist?"

Dennis nodded.

"I'd say yes. I'd like to know why she thinks that. Does her captain have the evidence she presented to him?"

"He said he looked at it and handed it back to her. Told her to stop pursuing something that wasn't there. When she refused to let it go and investigated after hours, he put her on leave until she worked through her issues."

"I don't know, Dennis. The drug raid incident…" Kyle choked on the words. "And her cousin's death so close together might have sent her into a tailspin. I haven't talked to her since the day before the explosion that killed Amber, so I'm not sure I can make that leap."

His boss raised a brow and narrowed his gaze.

"Don't look at me like that." Kyle glared back.

"Like what?"

It appeared that Dennis planned to shift from boss to friend. Kyle refused to take the bait. He waved a hand, brushing off the question. "I'll get her statement about tonight and have it ready for you midmorning."

"Actually, I'm putting you in charge of Detective Bowman. I want you to stay with her and see her safely to a hotel room once she's discharged."

"What?" Kyle's voice rose. The man couldn't be serious.

"And yes, I'm serious."

Had he said that out loud, or had the sheriff started reading minds? "I didn't say anything."

"You didn't have to. It's written all over your face."

Sometimes it really stunk having an intuitive boss. Kyle crossed his arms. "Fine. I'll get her statement, stay with her and see her to the hotel."

Dennis smiled. "Thank you."

"Stupid babysitting job," Kyle muttered.

"Excuse me. I didn't hear you."

"Right." Now the man thought he was funny.

"Kyle." Dennis turned serious. "She's a fellow officer and needs our help until her memory returns. Plus, I think it's time you let go of your hurt and move on. From what you've told me, in my opinion, you need to clear the air between you and Cassidy before that can happen."

He'd told Dennis more about the death of his fiancée than anyone else in town. The man had a way of tugging information from you. Which might have something to do with the fact he was a great listener and compassionate guy. Kyle had never seen his friend riled except for when he met his wife a little over eight months ago. That had been interesting to watch. The calm and easygoing man had let his emotions out. It had shocked yet comforted him to know Dennis wasn't perfect.

Kyle sighed. "I'm not sure I agree with you, but I'll do what you've requested."

Dennis patted his shoulder. "That's all I ask."

"Detective Howard."

Kyle shifted his attention to the gray-haired doctor standing in the archway of the room. "Yes, sir." He stood and strode toward the man.

"We transferred Ms. Bowman to a room a little while ago."

Sheriff Monroe joined them. "How's she doing?"

"Still a bit foggy. She remembers her name and job and little things about her life. But isn't clear beyond that."

"Will she regain her full memory?" Kyle had called her a friend once upon a time, but he'd walked away. He wasn't prepared for the concern for her well-being that struck him in that moment.

The doctor nodded. "I believe she will. The concussion is mild. But she needs time to heal."

"When can we see her?" Dennis asked.

"You can go in now, but please don't disturb her if she's asleep. And don't hound her for answers she can't give." The doctor pinned them both with a stern look.

Kyle stuffed his hands in his pockets. "Wouldn't dream of it."

The doctor snorted. "Room 202. And my nurses have orders to throw you out if you cause a problem." With that, the man spun and walked away.

Kyle's mouth hung open. He shifted to his boss. "What did I do to deserve that?"

"Well, the last person you brought in here caused a ruckus."

"That dude was drunker than a skunk when I arrested him. And he yelled at me, not the other way around."

Dennis chuckled.

"Not funny. I had to restrain the guy while the nurse stitched him up. And then the man threw up all over me."

"You obviously made an impression."

He glared at his boss, who coughed to cover his laugh.

"Go watch over Cassidy. Let me know if she recalls anything else."

"Sure." Kyle wanted to stomp off like a toddler, but he grabbed his jacket from the waiting room, straightened his spine and headed toward Cassidy's room. He could do this.

A few minutes later, he tapped on the door of room 202. No answer. He peeked in and found her sleeping. Kyle walked in, lowered himself into the easy chair near her bed and waited.

His emotions reminded him of one of those scrambler rides at the county fair. Too many directions to count. And a queasy stomach to go with it.

Cassidy had been Amber's best friend, and by default,

his too. The three of them hung out together frequently. He knew the woman lying in the bed better than most.

That's what made him wonder how she could have been so careless with Amber's life. It didn't matter that the explosion surprised everyone. Her raid—her responsibility.

He bunched his coat, tucked it behind his head as a pillow and closed his eyes.

God, why? I was finally getting a handle on my grief. The pain had dulled. Now that Cassidy is here, it's like someone filleted my heart. I'm going to need You to help me through this mess.

He breathed deep, pushing the tension from his body, and drifted off.

"Kyle?" Cassidy's soft voice roused him from a light sleep.

He hadn't realized how badly his body had craved rest until the dim lights and quiet room wrapped him in a cocoon. He sat up and wiped a hand down his face. "Yeah."

"What are you doing here?" The harsh rasp in her voice remained.

"The sheriff asked me to make sure you're okay."

She patted the back of her head and winced. "Ouch. What happened?"

His brows rose to his hairline. "You don't remember?"

"Not really."

Kyle resisted the overwhelming urge to move to her side and hold her hand. "Doc said it might take a while to regain your memory."

Cassidy nodded, then looked around the room. "Where's Amber?"

"Excuse me?" His breath caught in his throat.

"Amber. You know, my best friend. My partner."

She had to be joking. And it wasn't funny. "Amber's dead."

Cassidy looked at him like he'd grown donkey ears and a tail. "I…" Her eyes darted back and forth, mentally searching for answers. Tears welled. "The explosion."

He nodded.

She deflated against the bed. "And you've hated me ever since."

"*Hate* is such an ugly word," Kyle snipped.

"Well, what would you call it?" she challenged.

"I'm…angry." He felt his blood pressure rise, and before he stopped his words, they tumbled out. "You were the one in charge."

"We had no idea the guy had rigged the door to blow. There was no intel about the suspect using explosives." The soft beep of the heart monitor attached to Cassidy increased.

His ability to maintain a civil tone disappeared. "Maybe so, but you didn't even attend your best friend's funeral."

She threw back the blanket, uncovered her arms, exposing the scars he'd seen earlier, and held them up in plain view. "Because I was in the hospital recovering from burns and vertigo from the blast. And you would have known that if you'd taken the time to come visit me." Cassidy rubbed her forehead. "I thought you were my friend." Her voice had lost its bite.

Guilt flooded Kyle, but he couldn't get past blaming Cassidy for Amber's death.

Maybe he'd failed in the friend department, but she'd failed as Amber's partner.

Cassidy's scars itched at Kyle's accusations. The memory of the raid and her friend's death hung huge above her head, but beyond the basics, she'd blocked out the details of that day to keep her sanity. The report said Amber breached the entry before Cassidy gave the orders, and the door exploded on contact. For the life of her, she couldn't remember the specifics.

The weight of the Kevlar and the smell of smoke filled her senses. The heat of the fire pricked her skin. The world spun out of control. And the odor of burnt skin—her skin—roiled her stomach.

Sweat beaded on Cassidy's forehead. Air refused to enter her lungs. She struggled to force the memory away, but it hung on.

"Cassidy?"

With a shaky hand, she retrieved her water from the roller table and took a sip. The cool liquid coated her throat, chasing away the acidic burn. After returning her cup, she eased back against her pillow and wiped the perspiration from her upper lip.

"Sorry." The flashbacks had dwindled over time, but she had a feeling they'd return with an unwanted frequency after facing another fire.

Kyle leaned forward and clasped his hands between his knees. "Let's start with what you do remember."

She rubbed her forehead to ease the ache. "After my cousin Laura's death, my supervisor forced me to take an extended leave."

"Why?"

Because he thinks I've lost my mind. "He thought I needed to take time off to deal with the losses after the failed raid and Laura's death." The peek into her cousin's accident had sent her on a search for the truth, but, at the moment, the reasons eluded her.

"And Valley Springs was your choice of locations to recover…" He used air quotes around *recover* and drew out the word.

"To be honest, I don't recall why." Cassidy wanted to open her brain and scoop out the information. The doctor told her to give it time. Patience. Not one of her strengths. Solving problems and reaching goals—that's where she excelled.

"What about last night? Anything you can tell me is appreciated." Kyle slipped a notebook and pen from his pocket. "Sheriff Monroe promised the fire captain I'd get your statement."

Of course, they needed her statement. She smoothed the wrinkle in her blanket and straightened the cup and tissue box on the small table. Hands folded in her lap, she returned her focus to Kyle. "I'll try to help any way I can, but the events are a little foggy."

"Anything you can tell me is fine."

She searched her memory for the events of last night. "I sat by the fireplace reading most of the evening."

"Was the book any good?"

"It wasn't a book." She scrunched her forehead and stared at the wall. "I don't recall what, though."

"Did you have anything to eat or drink right before the fire?"

The strange question jerked her gaze to him. "Not that I remember."

"Are you sure?" The skeptical look in his eyes made her wonder what he suspected.

"Am I sure about anything right now? No."

He scowled while he jotted in his notebook.

Cassidy fisted the blanket. Dread knotted in her stomach. "Kyle, what's going on?"

He looked at her and pursed his lips. His gaze never wavered.

Too tired to play games, she wanted the truth. "What are you trying to say?"

"Fine. The fire captain found prescription pills in your apartment."

Cassidy hadn't wanted to admit her problem with insomnia and the nightmares that woke her multiple times a night…a sign of weakness she had no desire to confess. A weakness her father would shame her for. She sighed. "They're mine. I've had a few problems sleeping since the explosion. The doctor prescribed them to help me sleep."

"Well, that answers one question." Kyle exhaled.

"And what's the other?" She hadn't liked his tone. Even though he looked as though he'd aged ten years in the past nine months, she refused to allow him to crawl beneath her defenses.

He shifted on the chair. His expression hardened.

The man had an attitude, and she didn't feel like putting up with his judgment. Her head hurt, and the scars on her arm ached where they'd turned pink and tender from the heat. "Spit it out."

"When did you start drinking?"

"What?" Now she was really confused. "You know I don't drink. And you know why."

He tapped the pen on his knee. "That's what I'd thought, but the evidence says different."

"I don't understand. What evidence?" Where had he gotten that idea?

He tilted his head and raised a brow.

"Seriously, Kyle. You need to explain." She didn't have the energy to put up with his condemnation.

His shoulders drooped. "They discovered a broken wine bottle near where I found you."

How could that be? She shook her head and regretted the movement. "Sleeping prescription, yes. Wine. No way. I wouldn't do that."

"The old you—I agree. I don't know the new you."

"And whose fault is that?" she bit out. His negativity toward her had pushed her limits. "What did I do to you?

Amber's death was terrible. I miss her every day. But it wasn't my fault." If only her heart agreed. She'd replayed every decision and plan about the raid. All of it was tactically sound except for those last few seconds, which remained a mystery.

"Wasn't it? You were in command. You gave the order to breach."

"Then you didn't read the report. Amber hit the door before I gave the order." Cassidy suffered from a tremendous amount of guilt. Yes, she'd commanded the raid. Her team—her responsibility. She refused to admit that to Kyle, but in the end, Amber had moved prematurely, according to her teammates.

"She'd never be that careless."

Wow, his opinion of her was lower than she'd thought. "And I would?"

He all but glared at her.

"Never mind." Cassidy had her fill of his accusations. "You have my statement. Just go."

"No can do." Kyle sat back and crossed his arms.

"And why on earth not?"

"I promised the sheriff I'd see you to the hotel once the doctor releases you."

"Then I suggest you go find him and encourage him to discharge me so you can be relieved of your duties."

He opened his mouth, then closed it. "Fine. I'll be back." Kyle stood, paused by her bed like he intended to say something, then shook his head and exited the room.

Cassidy took five deep breaths. The tension bled off her, and she refocused her thoughts.

First things first. Regain her memory from last night and figure out why she chose Valley Springs, knowing Kyle lived there. And do all that without his judgment.

Right. Like that would happen.

She closed her eyes and tried to put aside the past—and failed.

The room phone rang, and Cassidy rolled to grab it. She groaned. Her muscles had stiffened, and her head protested the movement. She picked up the receiver. "Hello."

When no one answered, she tried again.

Breathing filled her ear. Not the creepy heavy kind like in a horror movie, but disturbing all the same. The person wanted her to know he was on the line. But to what end?

"I know you're there."

"Hello, Detective Bowman."

The hairs stood on the back of her neck. "What do you want?"

"You. Your time is coming to an end." The whispered words sent the sensation of icy fingers creeping up her spine and onto her scalp.

Her mind spun to last night. Bits of memory flashed like short video clips. Sitting in her chair. Taking the sleeping medication. Hearing a noise. The shadowy figure. The pain in her head. The smell of smoke. His words *sweet dreams*.

She jolted upright and slammed the phone down.

Someone had done this to her, and he knew where to find her.

Her pulse raced, and air refused to fill her lungs. The increase of the heart monitor tunneled in her ears. Who had targeted her?

"What's wrong?"

Cassidy jerked her gaze to Kyle, who had returned and stood in the doorway. "He tried to kill me."

In two strides, Kyle stood by her bed. "Who?"

"The man who hit me over the head."

Kyle shook his head. "You fell onto the brick hearth."

"No, I didn't." She gritted her teeth.

"Cassidy. When I found you, I didn't see anyone around

except Mr. Webster. And the fire captain hasn't said anything about an intruder. Just the broken wine bottle and your prescription."

"I don't drink! Someone did this to me!"

Why wouldn't Kyle believe her?

TWO

The tentacles of fatigue wrapped around Cassidy and tugged her under. She forced her eyes open, fighting against the exhaustion, but the hum of the truck tires threatened to pull her back to sleep.

True to his word, Kyle had stayed until the doctor discharged her. While he waited for the completion of the paperwork, he'd investigated her mysterious caller. The hospital had a record of a call to Cassidy's room, but nothing indicated a phone number—most likely it was a burner phone.

At least Kyle believed her—this time.

He had yet to come around and acknowledge that someone had attacked her in the apartment, and that bothered her more than she wanted to admit. A year ago, she'd had his trust, but Amber's death had changed their friendship from amicable to nonexistent.

Once out of the hospital, she had insisted they see what remained of her temporary home before he dropped her at the hotel. But the short drive proved more challenging than she'd anticipated.

Her energy level continued to hover around zero, but she wanted to look for evidence that explained her presence in Valley Springs. Not to mention any clues to the person who'd tried to kill her.

The truck stopped, and she took a deep breath. Her gaze ran over the fire-damaged renovated garage. The front window had shattered, and her Christmas tree lay half in and half out of the opening. The stark contrast of her landlord's house with all the decorations compared to the blackened siding of her temporary home had a shocking effect.

"Are you ready?" Kyle draped his arm over the steering wheel and shifted to face her.

"Might as well get inside and see if my clothes survived." And hunt for proof of an intruder. She had no idea why it mattered so much, but she wanted people to think the best of her.

Kyle slipped from the vehicle and met her at the passenger side. Being forever the gentleman, even though he hated her, he opened her door.

Without a word, she swung her legs out and stood. She gripped the frame to steady herself. The day had already taken its toll. The first thing on the list as soon as she arrived at the hotel, a nap. But she refused to admit her limitation to Kyle. No reason to make him think less of her. "Is it safe to go in?"

Kyle stood beside the passenger door. "Captain Phillips assured me they'd put out the fire and had taken care of the hot spots. He released the scene a couple hours ago."

"Then let's get in there." The lingering odor of smoke caught in her throat, and a wave of panic washed over her. Her airway closed off. She coughed to ease the sensation.

"Maybe this isn't a good idea. I can gather your clothes, or if you prefer, I'll call Deputy Tara Fielding," Kyle offered.

No, thank you. Kyle digging through her personal things had awkward written all over it. And there was no reason to drag Tara over to do a job Cassidy could handle on her own.

"I'm good." Or she would be once she stuffed her reaction aside and proved Kyle wrong about the intruder. Several deep breaths later, Cassidy straightened her spine and strode to the front door. She entered the apartment with Kyle following close behind.

A Christmas tree corpse—the only thing left of her efforts to celebrate the holiday. She crossed the small distance from the entrance to the living room and ran her hand over the back of the easy chair. The pungent scent inside had glimpses of memory peeking through her muddled brain.

A memory of poring over documents flashed in her mind. She searched the end table for the files she'd studied last night. But came up empty. "Does Captain Phillips have my documents?"

"He didn't mention them, but I'll check." Kyle removed his phone and sent a text message.

The sensation of icy fingers traveled up Cassidy's spine. She jerked her gaze to the front window and peered through the cracked glass. Her years on the police force told her someone lurked outside—watching—waiting.

Nothing unusual caught her attention, but the feeling refused to subside. She made another scan of the surroundings. *Come on. Show yourself.* Just a glimpse of him was all she needed.

"What are you looking at?"

She glanced at Kyle. That was a good question. Her gaze drifted back to the street. The impression had disappeared.

"Nothing." Maybe she'd imagined it—fat chance.

Cassidy's skin crawled at the apartment's disarray. More than anything, she wanted to clean the mess, but instead, she stepped with care to the fireplace mantel, avoiding broken glass and debris.

She picked up the lone frame, charred on the edges. The

image of her cousin Laura stared back at her. The two of them stood, arms slung over each other's shoulders, grinning ear to ear after a doubles grass volleyball victory.

The photo brought a sad smile to her lips. No more hanging out with her cousin playing in volleyball tournaments, or going to baseball games together. Two of their favorite pastimes.

A memory niggled at her brain. She closed her eyes, hoping the thought coalesced. What had the missing files contained? She lifted the frame and stared at the picture. "I was investigating Laura's death."

She felt him move closer. "It was an accident."

She shook her head. "No, it wasn't."

"Cassidy."

How dare he! She turned and glared at him. "Don't take that tone with me. I know my cousin. She didn't drink. I don't drink. And you know why." Why did he have to think the worst of her?

She inhaled, calming her battered nerves. "Last night, I sat in that chair." She pointed to the recliner. "And pored over her file, looking for evidence to who killed her."

Kyle's phone dinged. He pulled it from his pocket and read it. "No documents were found."

Cassidy hadn't made it up. She'd laid the case files on the table. So, where were they? "He must have taken them."

"Who?"

She patted the back of her head near her stitches. "The guy who clocked me."

Kyle huffed a sigh.

"I know you don't believe me, but it's the truth." She clutched the photo to her chest and spun away from him. Tears pricked her eyes as she strode to her bedroom. She'd lost in so many ways over the years. First, her mom to cancer when she was twelve, then her high school friend to a drunk driver a few years later, and soon after, her father was killed in action while on deployment. Now Amber and Laura.

She had no one left except her aunt and uncle, who lived half a country away. And they rarely visited even when Laura had been alive. Cassidy had counted on Kyle to help ease the grief after Amber's death, but he'd walked away, leaving her cousin to pick up the pieces. Then Laura was gone.

Even though she and Kyle had only been friends, the distance hurt. But the blame he'd dropped on her, that's what had taken her to her knees.

The hint of smoke trailed down the short hallway to her bedroom. She peered in and surveyed the room. A queen-size bed and two nightstands lined one wall with a mountain landscape picture as the focal point. A walk-in closet and ensuite bathroom entrance were on the other. The window positioned straight ahead had tan curtains that matched the forest green comforter. Not her taste, but the decor provided a calming effect.

The room had no damage, but the smoky smell lingered in there too. Her future included a trip to the laundromat. She placed the treasured picture on the bed and headed straight for the closet. She yanked down her carry-on suitcase and threw in several outfits to get by for a few days. Then moved to her nightstand and pulled open the drawer to retrieve her wallet and phone charger.

A set of keys lay inside. She scooped them up and examined them. Not car keys. She bit her lip, searching her memory for the answer. Wrapping her hand around the metal, she squeezed. What did they go to?

The knock on the head had scrambled her brains, but her most recent memories returned little by little. It was like trying to look through murky water and grab ahold of an object. Given time her mind would clear. But until then, she hated the uncertainty.

"What did you find?"

Cassidy jumped. Her hand flew to her chest. "Don't scare me like that."

Kyle leaned against the doorjamb with his arms folded, watching her. He pointed to her hands. "Well?"

"Keys." She dangled them from her finger.

"For what?"

"If you'll give me a minute, I'll see if I can figure that out." She ignored him and directed her attention to the keys.

Maybe a couple of smaller ones for a padlock or file cabinet and a larger one for a door. Not to the front door of the apartment. She was sure of that, but to where? The brain fog from her injury drove her nuts.

She prided herself on the structure and the attention to detail with which she approached life and work. A gift from her military father—a quality, good and bad. Some said she bordered on OCD. Cassidy didn't have obsessive-compulsive disorder. Tendencies? She hated to admit it, but that was a good possibility. But she had no doubt in her mind that she'd learned those *tendencies* during her youth. *Thank you, Dad.*

She shook off the direction of her thoughts and placed her cousin's photo in her suitcase. She froze. The answer, or at least part of it, teetered on the edge of her memory. All she had to do was grab it and yank it free. *Come on.* She snapped her fingers. "My office."

Kyle arched a brow. "Come again?"

"I rented a small office when I came to town." Relief flowed through her at the memories that had returned.

"Because?"

"I told you. Laura's death was not an accident. I also found other suspicious deaths in the area. But out of all the accidental or unsolved deaths in the region, I can't remember what made them special." Cassidy continued to place necessities into her bag with a precision that would please her father, and willed her brain to function.

"And you're investigating on the sly." The look of judgment from Kyle raised her hackles.

"Since my boss thinks I've lost touch with reality..." She gritted her teeth. "I'm not letting this go. Laura deserves better." She shoved the keys into her pocket, then slammed the top of her suitcase closed and zipped it shut.

Kyle remained quiet. He strode over and grabbed her bag. His gaze met hers. "Were those the files that are missing?"

"Copies of them." At least he hadn't completely brushed her off.

He blinked. "You have the originals?"

"I have a flash drive at my office with all the reports and scene photos."

"I don't know what to think, but since you are dead set on pursuing this, let's go retrieve the drive so you can print another set of documents."

"Really?" Had she heard him correctly? He was willing to help her reprint the files?

"Of course. I'm supposed to get you what you need and deliver you safely to the hotel. I think that falls into that category."

Her shoulders drooped. Right. Kyle was only doing his duty. She straightened, unwilling to let him see her disappointment. "Sounds good to me."

He nodded. "Sheriff Monroe secured a hotel room for you at the Sterling Inn. It's not fancy, but it's clean and comfortable. The owner is nice too."

"I appreciate his efforts. Please tell him thank you."

"He'll be checking in with you later, so you'll have the

opportunity to tell him in person." Kyle led the way to the truck. He placed her bag in the back of the extended cab and moved to the side, then motioned to the passenger seat.

She grabbed the door frame, hefted her exhausted body up and settled in. After grabbing the seat belt and clicking it into place, she stiffened.

The hair prickled on the back of her neck. Her gaze darted around the neighborhood. Her watcher was out there—again.

But she refused to tell Kyle. The man already doubted her. No need to add to his assumptions.

Kyle shut the passenger door and scanned the area. His years as a deputy had his hand hovering over his weapon. The unease that oozed from Cassidy bled off onto him.

She might have led the raid that killed Amber, but his fiancée had spoken highly of Cassidy's instinct as an officer. He wished it had translated to that fatal command. But today, his priority centered on her safety.

With one last look and nothing that triggered concern, he slipped behind the wheel. "What's the address to your office?"

"If you'll drop me off at the hotel, that'll be fine. I can check the office later."

He put the truck into gear. "Let's get your documents. Having those might help you put all the pieces together." The faster he figured out what Cassidy thought she'd discovered, the better.

She considered him for a moment, then nodded. "Three twenty-four North Elm."

Kyle pulled away from the fire-damaged apartment and headed toward downtown. The address seemed familiar. "Isn't that the bakery?"

"I rented the space above the shop. The owner uses part

of it for storage, so the rent's cheap since I only needed the bedroom and access to the bathroom." Cassidy shifted and gazed out the passenger window.

Apparently, she had finished talking.

He took the hint and focused on his driving. But his mind refused to let go of the details that Cassidy gave him about last night.

Had someone really attacked her and set her apartment on fire? He hadn't found evidence to the fact. Then again, he wasn't an arson investigator, and with all the firefighters stomping through the living area, they would have destroyed it if anything did exist.

A few minutes later, he found a spot in front of Deb's Delights bakery and parked. "Is this okay, or do I need to pull around back?"

Cassidy snapped out of her trance. "This is fine. But we'll need to go to the side of the building. There's an exterior entrance I use."

He met her on the sidewalk, and they walked in silence around the corner and up the stairs.

She pulled the keys from her pocket and opened the door. "Come on in."

He entered behind her and took in the small space. The living area contained a love seat in the main part of the room, and neatly stacked boxes lined the wall under a window that faced the street. He squinted at the labels. Napkins. Paper plates. Paper cups. And who knew what Deb had stacked behind the first row.

Cassidy wasn't kidding when she said Deb used the place as a storage room. His gaze traveled to the small kitchen to his left. Two stools tucked under the breakfast bar offered a place to eat. A coffeemaker with a pod spinner next to it sat on the counter, and several coffee mugs hung on a cup tree. The adjacent countertop contained a microwave, and a dish strainer sat next to the sink. The area appeared functional and well-used.

The door snicked shut behind him.

"Follow me." Cassidy skirted around the love seat and strode down the short hall. "The bathroom is on the right, and the bedroom, aka my office, is here at the end." The keys jingled on her fingers until she found the right one. She unlocked the door.

Weird that the room had a lock on the outside. He almost chuckled at the strange places his cop brain went.

She glanced back at him and gave him a lopsided smile. "It's not what you're thinking."

"I didn't say anything." He bit back a grin.

"No, you didn't, but you were thinking it." She pushed the door open. "I asked Deb if I could add the extra security."

He nodded, surprised she'd read him so well. Kyle followed her in and jerked to a stop. Documents and photos covered an entire wall. Her own version of a murder board. He moved in for a closer look. Pictures of a car accident, a drowning in a lake, a drive-by shooting, a strangulation and a stabbing. Red strings connected many of the images to a question mark, but she'd linked the others together.

"I don't need those. I have it all on a flash drive and have pictures of the work." She waved at the wall.

Kyle watched her disappear under the desk that sat in the middle of the room. He studied the meticulous desktop and the bookcase next to it. Cassidy might have changed in certain ways over the last year, but her necessity for neatness had not.

The bottom of her boots stuck out from under the desk. What was up with her hiding the flash drive there? Was her boss correct? Had she lost her grip on reality?

He shrugged and shifted his attention to the wall. He

stepped closer and narrowed his gaze, studying the data. All different MOs and different victim types. Strange. And she thought a serial killer had done all of this? He turned toward her. "Interesting collection of cases."

"Yes." She scooted out from under the desk and held a small black thumb drive. "Got it." Cassidy stood, but her stilted movements spoke of the injuries she'd acquired last night. She gripped the edge of the desk to steady herself before brushing the invisible dust off her pants. "We can go now."

So much for gleaning more information from her. But it was probably for the better. Kyle wanted her safely tucked away and a quick end to his babysitting job.

"If you're ready, I'll take you to the hotel and get you settled."

She shrugged. "Whenever you are."

He motioned for her to go ahead. They stepped from her office, and she secured the office door.

They exited the apartment. Cassidy locked up and headed down the steps.

She froze.

He clutched the rail to stop himself from plowing into her and pushing her down the stairs.

Her hand went to where a weapon normally sat on her hip.

Kyle mimicked her movement and drew his Glock, holding it next to his leg. Ready to aim. "What's wrong?"

After scanning her surroundings, she exhaled. Her white-knuckle grip on the rail released. Her fingers trembled as she covered her mouth. "Nothing." Without another word, she continued her trek down the stairs.

Right. That's why her cop instincts had kicked in, and her hands shook. Then again, her boss put her on forced leave due to emotional reasons. Kyle slid his gun into his holster and followed Cassidy to the truck, wondering what he should believe about the woman who used to be his friend.

"Sorry about that. The fire has me on edge." She got into the passenger side and shut the door.

On edge? More like a startled deer with semis coming from both directions. He climbed into the driver's side and cranked the engine. "Understandable. I'll get you to the hotel so you can rest." *And I can put this whole thing behind me and pretend you don't exist.* Cruel—yes. And he had to work on that. God expected more from him, but the hurt and anger had seeped in, and it was all he could do to be civil to Cassidy, whose poor judgment had killed the woman he'd loved.

What about what you did?

No, he refused to go there. He shook off the self-incriminating thoughts and pulled from the parking spot.

Five minutes later, Kyle entered the lot at the hotel where Sheriff Monroe had arranged a room for Cassidy and parked near the entrance.

"No need to get out. I'll take it from here." She reached for the door handle.

"Are you sure?" Not that he really wanted to go in, but his conscience had tugged at him to play nice.

"Positive." Cassidy slipped from the truck and retrieved her suitcase. "Thanks for everything."

Arm resting over the back of the seat, Kyle shifted to face her. "No problem."

Hand on the door, ready to slam it shut, she halted. "Listen. I know you're not my biggest fan, but I do appreciate all you've done." She scraped her bottom lip with her teeth. "I miss our friendship." The passenger door clicked shut. After a quick glance over her shoulder, she strode into the building.

What would Amber say about his attitude toward Cassidy?

Nope. He didn't want to go there. It was easier to maintain his current status of hurt. Throwing the responsibility onto her gave him somewhere to lay blame—away from him. Time to call his boss before he did something stupid like forgive Cassidy. He hit Dennis's speed dial number.

"Monroe."

"Hey, boss." He drummed his fingers on the steering wheel. The red poinsettias near the entrance threw him back to last year. Amber loved the holiday plant. She'd buy six or seven for her apartment every Christmas.

"Kyle. How are things going?"

He shook off the direction his mind had gone. "I delivered Detective Bowman to the hotel, so my babysitting job is officially over."

"Detective Bowman, huh?"

"Yeah, what about it?" Sometimes having your boss as a friend stunk.

Dennis sighed. "Did you give Cassidy your business card with your phone number?"

He had to be kidding. He'd changed his number, so she couldn't call him. "No."

"Kyle. I know there's a painful past involved, but don't let that cloud your judgment."

"Are you talking to me as a friend or my boss?" He clenched his teeth tight enough that his jaw hurt.

"Do I really have to make it an order?"

Sometimes he wanted to wring the man's neck for pointing out the truth. "Fine. I'll go give it to her."

"Smart man."

Kyle hung up, then yanked out his wallet, retrieved his business card and jotted down his cell number on the back. "Just how long do I have to be her keeper?"

He plodded into the hotel and to the front desk. The silver-haired woman had her back to him. "Hi, Nancy."

Mrs. Sterling pivoted to face him. "Detective Howard, how are you?"

"I'm good. Listen, the woman that just came in is staying here on the sheriff's department dime, and I forgot to give her something. Could I get her room number?"

Nancy scowled at him. "You're pushing the rules, you know that."

He leaned against the counter and gave her his most innocent smile. "Please."

"Fine. But if she gets mad, it's on you. Room 227."

"Thank you. You're a gem."

"I can never say no to you boys." The older lady rolled her eyes and swatted at him. "Get out of here before I change my mind." It seemed as though the entire older population of Valley Springs claimed the sheriff and his detectives as their boys even though they were all in their thirties. However, he'd never minded. He enjoyed his role as honorary grandson to many.

Kyle stepped into the elevator and pushed the button for the second floor. He propped himself against the wall and tapped the business card on his thigh, debating if finding Cassidy and giving her his new phone number was a good idea. He'd changed it to avoid her contacting him after Amber's death. But trouble had found Cassidy, and he supposed the past shouldn't matter—but it did. His own guilt tugged at him.

Nope. Not going there.

If he allowed that door to open, he'd never get it shut.

The elevator dinged and its door slid open.

He pushed to stand and stepped from the elevator.

A scuffle down the hall grabbed his attention. His brain scrambled to process what was happening.

A man's arm wrapped Cassidy's throat from behind, lifting her off the ground.

Her feet dangled in the air. She fought and clawed at the attacker's arm.

A faint "Help" reached Kyle's ears.

The momentary paralysis evaporated. "Cassidy!" He yanked his duty weapon and sprinted toward her. "Stop! Police!"

The man released her, and she tumbled to the floor. The assailant took off out the emergency stairway, the door banging shut behind the masked man.

Kyle wanted to chase after the guy, but Cassidy required his attention. He holstered his weapon, then grabbed his cell and placed a call to dispatch. "This is Detective Howard. Send backup and an ambulance to Sterling Inn. Suspect attacked Detective Bowman and escaped out the back."

"Copy that, Kyle. Help is on the way."

He hung up and dropped to his knees beside where Cassidy sat, leaning against the wall. "Are you okay?"

Wide watery eyes stared back at him. She clutched her throat, gasping for air. "Now do you believe that someone's trying to kill me?" she asked, her voice hoarse and barely above a whisper.

He never would have believed it if he hadn't seen it with his own eyes. Now? How could he ignore the facts in front of him?

Someone definitely wanted to eliminate her. But why?

He lifted her fingers from her throat. Red marks marred her skin where the man had attempted to strangle her. "The paramedics will be here soon. Try to take it easy until they arrive."

"Kyle." She grabbed his arm. The strength in her grip surprised him. She pulled him closer. Her icy blue eyes begged him to listen. "You have to believe me. You saw him. I'm not making this up."

The desperation in her words punched him in the gut. Sheriff Monroe's insistence that Kyle give her his phone number had saved her life.

A vision of Cassidy lying dead in the hotel hallway invaded his mind. He might be mad at her, but losing her because of his stubbornness left him reeling.

Whatever Cassidy had stumbled upon had made her a target. He couldn't deny what he had witnessed. "I believe you."

THREE

Cassidy struggled to her feet. *He actually believed her?* Kyle's admission had stolen what little breath she had left.

The hotel carpet's red-and-blue twisty diamond pattern sent nausea swirling in Cassidy's belly. Dizziness due to lack of oxygen lingered, and the reality of what happened settled in. The hallway tunneled and closed in on her. Her legs wobbled. She placed a hand on the wall to steady herself.

A detective did not fall apart in front of others. Especially at a crime scene. It didn't matter that the attempted murder was hers. She filled her lungs, then shifted and leaned against the wall for support.

She appreciated the men and women doing their job but hated the title of victim. And more than anything, she despised the looks of pity they flashed at her as they walked past.

Her fingers went to her throat. The bruises ached, and the gash on the back of her head from last night's attack throbbed in time with her heartbeat, reminding her that the man she believed to be a serial killer had her in his sights.

What had she stumbled upon to garner the killer's attention?

The lack of memory annoyed her, but at least it had improved since she'd left the hospital. A haze remained, but only bits and pieces hadn't materialized.

Kyle strolled over. "Doing okay?"

"Sure," she croaked. Lovely. She sounded wonderful—not.

"Cassidy." His tone made her pause. A cross between a warning and a semblance of caring. But she knew better. The man barely tolerated her.

To his credit, he'd stayed by her side after her attacker escaped. "Give me a little while. I'll be fine." And she would be—as soon as she knew what she'd stumbled upon to cause the killer to target her.

Kyle raised his hand as if to touch her bruises but withdrew it before he made contact. "The paramedics will be here soon."

"I don't need them." She'd had enough of hospitals to last a lifetime.

He crossed his arms. "I'm not debating this with you. It's the paramedics or the hospital. You choose."

"Fine. I'll agree to the paramedics, but that's as far as it goes. No hospital." If her body allowed her to stand tall, she'd meet his determined stance, but she had to settle for stern words.

He scowled but nodded.

The knot in her stomach eased. She'd won the battle. The first of many to come—she had no doubts about that.

By sheer will, she remained upright. The man had the ability to annoy even the most patient person. She closed her eyes for a moment and inhaled, calming her mind. Maybe accepting medical help wasn't such a bad idea after all.

The elevator door opened, and two men stepped off.

Cassidy's heart rate ratcheted. Under normal circumstances, she'd prepare to face danger head-on. Today, the urge to cower hit her hard.

Kyle rested a hand on her forearm. "Relax. That's my boss and partner."

She blew out a breath between pursed lips. The overwhelming reactions since her attack had to stop. Daddy never allowed weakness. Good thing he couldn't see her now. He'd be disappointed.

"Howard."

"Hang tight. I'll be right back." Kyle strode off and joined the men. "Sheriff Monroe."

Her pulse rate slowed. One would think that the law enforcement officers roaming the hall would give her a sense of security, but in reality—not so much. She had to get it together and act like the detective she was. The last thing she needed was Kyle questioning her abilities even more than he already did.

He stood in a deep discussion with his boss and his partner, who she recognized from the hospital but hadn't met yet. If the glances in her direction were any indication, she was the topic. Great.

She exhaled. She refused to allow her attacker and the negative opinion of others to control her responses. If only her brain would engage. The answer to this mess rattled around in there somewhere. Leaning against the wall, she gathered her strength and straightened as the three men strode toward her.

Sheriff Monroe nodded in greeting. "Nice to see you again, Detective Bowman. But I *am* sorry for the circumstances."

She pushed to a full standing position. Her legs threatened to give way, but she fought for control. "Thank you, sir."

"Please. Make it Dennis."

"All right then, Dennis. As long as you call me Cassidy."

"Done."

Kyle gestured to the other man. "This is my partner, Detective Doug Olsen."

"Doug. Please." Olsen held out his hand.

Cassidy shook it. "Nice to actually meet you."

Dennis opened his stance and crossed his arms over his chest. His easygoing manner switched to all business. "I'm aware you've given your statement to Kyle, but if you'll indulge me, I'd like to hear it firsthand."

So, this is what a witness to a crime endured. Cassidy had never been on the receiving end. She had a new appreciation for the frustration. The last thing she wanted to do was relive the assault.

Her hand moved of its own accord to her throat. "Kyle dropped me off at the entrance, and I checked into the hotel. I took the elevator to this floor. I didn't see anyone in the hallway, so I went to my assigned room. Before I tapped my key card to the electronic reader, the stairway door opened. The next thing I knew, a man spun me around and wrapped his hands around my neck. If Kyle hadn't decided to come find me…" She swallowed. Pain shot through her throat. She closed her eyes, willing the sting away.

"I'm sorry you had to go through all that." She opened her eyes and caught Dennis's gaze shift to Kyle and back to her. "Did you get a good look at the guy?"

She shook her head. "He's around six foot tall. Two hundred pounds, maybe. He wore a ski mask. But…" Cassidy searched her memory. "His eyes."

"What about them?" Kyle urged her to continue.

"I'm not sure how to explain it. They were hollow—lifeless."

The men stood there, staring at her. Wow, with all her training, an approximate height, weight and lifeless eyes were the only description?

Dennis cleared his throat. "While you were in the hospital, I had a chat with your supervisor."

Oh, great. She crossed her arms, mimicking the sheriff's stance. "So, you think I'm bananas too?"

The sheriff's eyes narrowed, and he studied her long enough she had to resist the urge to squirm. "I'm not ready to take your word for it that there's a serial killer on the loose, but I can't say I agree with your boss either."

"So, you don't think I'm on the edge, ready to fall apart at any moment?" Cassidy should tone it down, but the past twenty-four hours had her in a snippy mood. "Sorry. You could say I'm a bit—"

"Cranky. Tired. In pain. Concerned. Maybe even a little afraid." Kyle's eyebrow rose, challenging her.

In the past, she'd never agree. Her pride, cultivated by her father, tended to come forward, but Kyle had hit the target. She might as well admit it. "Yes, to all of those."

"And you have every right to be." Dennis glared at Kyle, then shifted his gaze to her.

She aimed her question at the sheriff. She had to know where the man stood on his opinion of her. "You don't think I'm losing my mind?"

"No. I don't. The threat to you is obviously real." The sheriff gestured to her neck. "I'd like to hear more about what you've found in your investigation and make my own conclusion."

Her jaw dropped. Had the attack messed up her hearing, or had Dennis said he'd listen to her findings?

The sheriff chuckled. "Yes, you heard me right."

Okay, that was creepy. Had the man read her mind?

Dennis turned his attention to Kyle and Doug. "I want the two of you to take Cassidy to a safe house. Better yet, if Doug is willing, take her to his place. She'll have better protection there than at a random location."

"Not a problem, boss. I have a couple of extra bedrooms, and you know the security is top-notch," Doug said.

"Kyle, you're to stick with Cassidy until we figure out what is going on."

"Dennis, I'm not sure that's a good idea," Kyle protested.

"Not up for discussion." Dennis's words came with a punch of authority.

"Yes, sir," Kyle responded with the respect of a deputy.

Dennis shifted his attention to her and softened his tone. "Once the paramedics examine your injuries, Kyle will escort you to Doug's place. Please let me know if you need anything. I'll check in with y'all later to see how things are going." With that, the sheriff turned and left.

"I…uh… Wait. What just happened?" If Cassidy wasn't mistaken, the sheriff had just ordered her to accept medical help and placed her in protective custody.

Doug snickered. "Welcome to the Anderson County Sheriff's Department and your first experience with Sheriff Dennis Monroe."

Kyle backhanded Doug's chest. "Ignore my partner. He thinks he's funny."

"Your boss is a force to be reckoned with, except without the force." Cassidy rubbed her forehead. "Does that even make sense?"

"More than. He's a pretty chill guy, but when he decides to act, watch out, it'll catch you by surprise," Kyle said.

Cassidy was grateful for the sheriff's willingness to listen to her, but she hadn't planned on having bodyguards.

Kyle motioned toward the elevator. "Let's get you out of here. We'll meet Ethan and Brent in the lobby."

"Who?"

"The paramedics. Then I'll take you to Doug's." Kyle retrieved her suitcase and motioned her toward the elevator.

Moments later in the lobby, the paramedics ushered her to a chair.

Brent introduced himself and his partner, then wrapped the blood pressure cuff around her arm. "Any other injuries besides the obvious?"

The cuff clamped down, and she winced at the tightness. "Maybe a few bruises where he grabbed me and slammed me against the wall, but other than that, I don't think so." When he released the pressure from the cuff, she squeezed her hand to relieve the ache.

Ethan examined her cheek, and she jerked away.

"Sorry." He eased his touch.

She hadn't realized the attacker had hit her.

Ethan moved his fingers to the marks where her assailant had attempted to strangle her. "It doesn't feel serious, but it'll be sore for a while."

She gritted her teeth. Not so much from the pain but from the idea that someone else had his hands on her neck.

When he moved away, she blew out a long breath. One more trauma to add to her long list over the past year.

The paramedics gave her the spiel about going to the hospital, but she declined and signed the papers for refusal to be transported.

"Thank you for your help." Cassidy did appreciate their kindness and medical advice but had no intention of letting them talk her into another hospital stay.

Brent slung the duffel over his shoulder. "Give us a call if you need anything."

She smiled. "Is that part of Valley Springs Fire Department service?"

"No, it's that of a friend."

Cassidy blinked. "But I just met you. You don't know me."

Ethan stepped forward. "You're a friend of these guys."

He jerked a thumb over his shoulder, indicating Kyle and Doug. "So, you're a friend of ours."

Friend? She and Kyle were hardly close anymore. But she let it go and accepted the gesture. "Thank you."

Brent slapped Kyle on the back and said goodbye.

Kyle joined her. "Ready to go?"

"I think so." She pushed out of the chair and groaned. "Sitting down was a bad move."

"We'll take it slow, but I want you in the truck A-Sap." Kyle switched to work mode.

"Then let's do this." Cassidy forced her legs to cooperate and headed to the front door of the lobby.

Once they exited the building, Kyle and Doug flanked her on either side. She'd accept it for now. Her body demanded it. But if they treated her like a delicate flower, they'd have words. Her daddy didn't raise a weak girl.

Kyle opened the passenger door to his truck.

She stared at the height of the step of his vehicle and sighed. If she wouldn't look ridiculous, she'd crawl into the seat.

"Come on. I'll help." Kyle took her arm and assisted her into the truck.

Much longer, and she'd fall asleep where she sat. "I know I keep saying this, but thank you."

"Not a problem." He shut the door, and Doug positioned himself in front of the passenger window while Kyle skirted the vehicle and got in the driver's side.

With a wave, Doug jogged to his SUV.

Kyle started the engine and waited for his partner to get to his vehicle. The man had gone from angry to helpful to quiet. His set jaw made her wonder what direction his emotions would go in next. The only word that described the circumstances—awkward.

Cassidy hated the silence between them and longed

for the easygoing friendship they'd once had. Kyle had visited her and Amber's apartment when he had time off. The three of them used to laugh and tease. Now—nothing.

She shifted to face him, searching for a safe topic. "I can't believe you guys are so casual with the sheriff. My boss would have our heads on a platter if we addressed him with anything but ultimate respect."

"That's Dennis for you. He's a good friend and a great boss." Kyle exited the parking lot. "It's an unusual situation."

"What do you mean?"

"Dennis is only a few years older than his detectives. We all hang out together. Go to church together. Makes for an interesting work environment. But we respect him and know when to switch into professional mode and treat him like the sheriff he is."

"Sounds like you all make a great team."

"We do. And we always have each other's backs." His gaze flicked to her, then back to the road.

She flinched. The dig had hit its mark. Two days ago, even yesterday, she would have fought back at the implication. Today, she didn't have the energy to continue the ongoing battle. And truthfully, she wanted it to stop. She missed his friendship.

Her gaze drifted to the passing scenery. She had no intentions of pushing. More pressing matters required her attention, like convincing Kyle that a serial killer existed and that her cousin had been murdered.

"Someday, we need to talk about the raid. But not today." She hoped she lived long enough to have that conversation.

Kyle knew he had to stop throwing the past in her face. How could one woman toss him into such turmoil?

Dennis was right. Kyle had never found closure, and deep down, he knew forgiveness was the key. But she'd opened the old wounds that he wanted to let fester.

Maybe the time had come for him to let go and heal. But forgiving Cassidy felt like a betrayal to Amber, plus he'd have to admit his own actions that had left guilt twisting his gut—his final words to Amber the morning of her death.

His cell phone rang. Doug's name flashed on the car display. Kyle tapped the answer button. "What's up?"

"Dark blue sedan four cars back."

Kyle peered out the rearview mirror and spotted the vehicle his partner had tagged. "I see it."

Cassidy straightened in her seat. "Me too."

"Plan?" Kyle tightened his grip on the steering wheel. He had to quit letting his mind spin about the past. He had a job to do, and his lack of focus could have deadly consequences.

"Speed up. Take the long way. I'll slow him down. As of now, I have no reason to stop him," Doug said.

"Got it." Kyle hung up.

Doug passed the offending car, slipped in behind Kyle's truck, and slowed, blocking the sedan.

Kyle pressed on the gas. Two blocks later, he turned right down a side street. Then made an immediate left. He made a continuous sweep of the road behind him and peered down the side streets as they drove past. So far, so good.

Several turns later, he released his death grip on the steering wheel. He stretched his neck from side to side, relieving the tension that had built in his muscles.

"You think we lost him?"

A glance at Cassidy revealed her alarm over the situation. She'd squeezed her hands together tight enough that her fingers turned white. Her coworkers called her the ice queen. The woman had more courage than her entire team. He'd never seen anything rattle her like this before.

He tucked away the information to ponder later and double-checked his mirrors. "Doug will work the problem, and I'll get you hidden away at his place."

She nodded, then leaned over the back of the seat and searched through the side pocket of her suitcase. When she settled back in, he noticed a Glock in her hand.

He looked at her and raised a brow.

"My backup piece since the sheriff has my duty weapon." She shrugged. "Just want to be prepared."

"Good thinking." Unless she decided to turn it on him for how he'd treated her. A smile tugged at his lips. The old Cassidy would threaten and tease him. But those days had passed. And he knew who to blame—himself. Another mistake in a long list of blunders.

Kyle wove through the residential streets of town. When confident that no one followed, he headed to Doug's. Ten minutes later, he pulled into the driveway and parked at the side of the house, out of sight from the street. He glanced at Cassidy, who sat motionless in the passenger seat, staring out at the backyard with unseeing eyes.

He gently jostled her shoulder. "We're here."

She blinked. "Sorry, I zoned out there for a bit."

"You've had a long day." His heart tugged at him for the woman who'd once been his friend.

"That's an understatement."

He chuckled and opened his door. "I'll grab your things. Let's get you inside."

She unbuckled and tucked her weapon in the waistband of her jeans. "Sounds good to me."

He rounded the truck and waited for her to join him.

They stepped to the front door, and Kyle unlocked it.

"You have your partner's key? I thought we'd have to wait for Doug to get here."

"He gave me an extra so we'd have the ability to come and go as needed. But I've taken care of things for him before when he goes on vacation. Plus, we hang out, so I know his place as well as I do my own."

"I hope I'm not putting him out by staying here."

Kyle opened the door, punched in the security code and motioned her inside. "Doug's okay with it. His security is the best, so his house is perfect for our needs."

"What's up with his security system?" Cassidy stepped in and froze. "Wow."

He almost laughed at her expression. "Not what you expected?"

"This is not a bachelor pad." Her gaze roamed the living room. "It's homey." She stepped farther into the house. "And that Christmas tree."

Kyle had helped Doug with the fir a couple of weeks ago. The monstrous thing took up the entire corner of the room. Once he and Doug secured the tree, Kyle had left the decorating to his partner and escaped the holiday cheer.

The next time he came over, the Christmas tree looked like something out of a romance movie. Twinkling lights, gold ribbon and glass ornaments. If Kyle remembered correctly, the star on top had been a wedding gift from Doug's grandparents.

How did Doug do it? The holidays made Kyle's heart ache. He'd lost so much, but so had Doug. And the man never complained.

Kyle shut the door, flipped the lock and reengaged the alarm. "There's a reason for the interior design touch. I want to respect his privacy. There's more to the story, but I'll give you the basics."

"You don't have to. I don't want to pry."

Kyle considered for a moment whether or not to say anything. Better she know than not. "It'll keep you from touching an area you shouldn't."

Her gaze met his. "If you're sure."

"Doug is ex-army. He's a bit of a security specialist. Hence the state-of-the-art system." Kyle headed for the extra bedroom and motioned for her to follow. "He was married during his army days."

Cassidy's steps faltered. "Was?"

Kyle nodded. "Yes. While he was on deployment, Cara witnessed a drug deal that ended with two men dead. She agreed to give her eyewitness account and testify if needed. The next day someone broke into their home and killed her."

"That's horrible."

"It was. The police know who ordered the hit but don't have enough evidence to arrest the person or persons responsible. Doug shipped home the next day. He requested a discharge from the army, and they granted it. Soon after, he came to work for the ACSD." Kyle entered the bedroom and stepped aside, giving Cassidy room to join him.

She paused. Her eyes darted around the room. "This can't be the same house."

"It's not. When he moved to Valley Springs, he decorated it to match the house they shared. From what he tells me, it's not exactly the same. He's put his own personal touches on it over the years, but it's similar."

"That is both sad and sweet."

Kyle placed her suitcase next to the dresser. "This will be your room. Doug's is across the hall, and mine is the one we passed next to yours."

Cassidy tilted her head. "So, I'm sandwiched between the two of you."

"Something like that." The coziness between them in

the tight space made Kyle uncomfortable. The ease of their conversation surprised him, and he didn't like it. The idea of falling back into their friendship after the way he'd lost Amber sent his blood pressure rising.

He itched to go for a jog to relieve the stress building inside. Or maybe just go home and leave Cassidy's care to Doug. Anything to get away from her. But he refused to let her or Dennis down. No matter how painful her presence was. "You look as though you need a long nap. Go ahead and rest. Once you feel up to it, come on out, and we'll take a look at your files."

She closed her eyes and stood there.

After a minute without a response, he thought she'd fallen asleep standing up.

She inhaled. Her eyes opened, and she glanced around the room. "I'm good."

"Are you sure about that? You've had a rough day."

"If I lie down, I won't get up until tomorrow. It's better if I keep going."

Kyle wasn't so sure, but he wouldn't argue. "Then let's get to it."

They walked to the living room. Only the hum of the heater and the tick of the clock on the wall broke the silence.

He sat on the couch, leaving the recliner for her. "Want to tell me what all this is about?"

Cassidy collapsed onto the easy chair. Her shoulders drooped, and she stared at her hands. A few moments later, she turned her focus on him. "I'm not sure where to start."

"At the beginning." He raised a brow.

She tugged on the sleeves of her shirt, hiding her scars from him. "Are you sure you want me to go there?"

Did he? Not really, but what choice did he have? Hiding from the past hadn't worked so far. "Might as well."

An engine rumbled outside.

Kyle held up a hand and pulled the weapon from his holster. He hurried to the door and peered through the blinds.

"Who is it?" Cassidy's voice quivered.

A familiar black SUV parked behind his truck.

He let out a long breath and reholstered his Glock. "Doug's here." Kyle let his partner in. "I take it you lost him."

Doug entered, took care of the alarm and hung his coat on the hook. "Of course." He turned to Cassidy. "Welcome."

"Thank you for letting me stay."

Doug waved her off. "I'll go make some coffee."

Kyle watched him leave the room. "He's not much for conversation, but he's a great partner."

"I trust you."

Kyle halted. She did? After the way he'd treated her? "Well…thank you."

Her smile told him she'd known her response had thrown him for a loop.

Kyle resumed his position on the couch and cleared his throat. "Let's get down to business."

Disappointment flashed across her face. "Right." Cassidy tucked her legs under her. "I'll give you an overview. After that, if you believe me, we can dig deeper."

Doug brought them each a cup of coffee and deposited a sugar-and-cream set on the table in front of them. He sat on the other side of the couch opposite Kyle and rested his ankle on his knee.

Cassidy narrowed her gaze, studied Doug for a moment, then refocused on Kyle. "You know that my cousin Laura died in a drunk driving accident." She used air quotes on the phrase *drunk driving*. "Which is impossible, but we'll get to that later."

A year ago, Kyle would've agreed with her and helped

her investigate. He had no reason to believe that Laura had changed. And the thought startled him. He'd made assumptions based on his perception of Cassidy. Which had nothing to do with Laura. He made a mental note to pull the copy of the accident and autopsy report he'd procured from VSPD and take another look.

"The information I collected from Valley Springs PD about Laura didn't help. I couldn't argue the blood alcohol level. I didn't understand it, but I had nothing to prove it was wrong, so I went a different path. Between my access to records due to my position with Brentwood PD and persuading the different police departments across the region to share what they had, I started looking into unsolved homicides and accidents where the families disagreed with the results of the investigation." She shrugged. "At that point, I *was* grasping for answers. But what I found had me taking a closer look."

"What did you find?" Kyle held his sarcasm at bay and decided to give her an opportunity to explain.

"Accidents without solid explanations. Homicides that had no evidence, or evidence that went against common sense. And all the families disagreed with the findings."

"But—"

She held up a hand. "I know people don't want to believe the worst about a family member. But their arguments had a ring of truth to them. Similar to my cousin Laura's death. The more I investigated, the more certain I became that a serial killer was involved."

"How many did you find?" Doug rubbed his thumb along the rim of his coffee mug.

"After expanding my search to include multiple counties, I found twenty-one that interested me, but thirteen fit together in a way I'd never seen before."

Kyle leaned forward, placed his cup on the table and clasped his hands between his knees. "And how was that?"

She lifted her gaze to him. "I don't remember exactly."

"I understand your foggy memory, but we need more than an impression to start investigating a serial killer." Kyle wasn't sure what to think at this point. But he required more than her gut reaction.

Cassidy straightened and pinched her lips. "Then I guess I better convince you before the guy makes me one of his victims."

Kyle stared at her defiant posture.

The woman wasn't wrong on the account that someone had her in his sights. More than likely, someone from an old case who held a grudge had targeted her for putting him behind bars. But a serial killer—he doubted it.

However, they had to find her attacker before he finished what he started.

FOUR

Cassidy's head ached. Not only from the lump on her head but from the hot/cold vibes she got from Kyle. He'd stayed civil. But one minute, he appeared to accept her judgment, the next, he looked at her like she'd grown horns and a tail.

When would he listen to her and accept that she hadn't done anything wrong the day Amber died? Kyle's accusations after the raid had hurt. She'd had meticulous plans for the operation and followed protocol to the letter. The explosion had shocked everyone. The team had no way of knowing the suspect had rigged the door with C4.

She sighed and turned to Doug. "Do you have a printer?"

With an eyebrow raised, he peered over the coffee mug at his lips. "Sure do."

"May I print pictures and documents?" Cassidy withdrew a flash drive from her pocket and waved it.

"I'll get my laptop." Doug placed his cup on the coffee table and disappeared down the hall.

Kyle pointed to the device in her hand. "Is that the drive from your office?"

She nodded. "I have everything on here." She was grateful, now more than ever, for renting the little office and hiding the flash drive. If she'd kept it in her apartment, the killer would most likely have found and destroyed it. As it was, he'd stolen the copies of her documents.

Doug returned, typed in his password and handed her the laptop.

"Thanks." She inserted the flash drive and opened her files. One by one, she sent them to the printer. All the documents that were now printing had papered her office wall, but this was easier than taking them down and rehanging. In fact, the process might help her remember. Plus, she'd snapped several pictures of her murder board.

Kyle retrieved the reports and photos and laid them on the coffee table. "Where do you want to start?"

She organized the papers by law enforcement departments where she'd downloaded them from, taking extra care to make the stacks neat and tidy. "Since my brain is a little mushy, I'd like to look them over and see if it'll trigger my memory."

"Sounds like a plan." Kyle took his seat and waited patiently for her to study the documents and pass them on to him and Doug to review.

Half an hour later, Kyle stood and stretched. "I don't know about these cases. They're all different. Even if the accidents and suicides were homicides, there's no connection. Different MOs and different victim types."

"I have to agree with my partner." Doug perused a file. "There's nothing to hint at a serial killer."

She couldn't argue their position, but she knew something had caused her to latch on to the idea. She excelled at her job. Her father had made sure of that. The possibility of making a mistake that huge—no way.

"And these are all over the place. Few are in the same areas. There's no common hunting ground, so to speak." Kyle strode to the kitchen. When he returned, he filled their coffee mugs and placed the carafe on the table.

Cassidy thanked him, then lifted a document and scanned it, looking for something—anything—to trigger her memory. The cases *were* all over the place, as Kyle had said. She snapped her fingers. "That's it." She spun to face Doug. "Do you have a map of the region—a paper one?"

He pursed his lips and scratched his jaw. "You know, I think I do." He left the room and came back a few minutes later with the map, corkboard and a box of multicolored pushpins.

"That's perfect." She stood and helped him prop the corkboard on a couple of chairs. "Hand me the map. I'll hold it while you pin it to the board."

Once the map was on display, she grabbed the summaries of each crime and placed a pin at each location.

After the thirteenth pin, she glanced at Kyle, wondering what was rattling around in his mind. Was he humoring her, or was he listening and considering her theory?

He squinted at the map. "You're color coding."

She nodded. "Blue for homicides, red for suicides, green for accidents, and yellow for the cases that I don't believe belong, but I didn't want to exclude them without a solid reason." She finished and stood back, arms folded. The groupings. That's what her brain had latched on to.

Doug joined Kyle and gestured to the different clusters of pushpins. "I don't know, partner. Something does feel off." Doug crossed his arms and leaned in for a better look.

A jolt of satisfaction zipped through Cassidy. "That's what I'm talking about. The groupings are too unusual to dismiss." She pointed to the pattern. Sets of three or four deaths scattered across the map, covering the region. The groups became visible when she used a paper map and push pins.

"I agree it's uncommon, but I can't make the leap to serial killer." Kyle exhaled. "Did you interview the families and friends noted in the case files?"

"I hadn't gotten very far when my boss told me to stop

investigating and put me on leave. That's when I decided to come to Valley Springs and examine Laura's death." Cassidy tapped where her cousin's accident happened. "The location of her crash isn't within one of the clusters but right outside. Just like this one and this one." She pointed to the other outliers on the map.

"I might be able to swallow the pockets of cases as connecting somehow, but those not in the clusters…" Kyle shook his head. "I can't go there. At least not yet."

Doug stepped closer to the map and squinted at it. "Maybe." He exhaled. "The sheriff wants our recommendation on whether or not to help you investigate. At the moment, I'm not inclined to give him a yes. But I'm intrigued by your analysis. So, keep talking, Cassidy. Convince me."

It all came down to her words. But they were listening. She examined the pushpins dotting the map. "I'll start with my cousin Laura. I know…knew…her. She didn't drink. Not to say she judged people who do, but when we lost our high school friend to a drunk driver, we made a pact to never touch the stuff." She twirled a piece of hair between her fingers. "I can't say it's always been easy, especially in college, but all we had to do was remember our friend and the awful way she died."

Cassidy closed her eyes, reliving the horrors of that night. She and Laura had witnessed the whole thing. Her friend Kate left Cassidy's house and stopped at the four-way stop at the end of the street. She'd given them a quick wave out the window and drove into the intersection. A drunk driver ran the stop sign going three times the speed limit, and plowed into Kate's car. Cassidy and Laura called 911 and ran to help. She'd crawled through the passenger side. Blood poured from Kate's head. She'd held Kate in her arms, praying for the paramedics to hurry. Moments later, her friend was gone.

She swiped at a tear that had escaped. "There's no way Laura had touched alcohol. Let alone been drunk."

"I've seen the preliminary autopsy report. She had a blood alcohol of .20. I'm not even sure how she drove at that point," Kyle said.

"Exactly. Plus, since she didn't drink, it would hit her harder." Cassidy prayed Kyle and Doug saw the inconsistencies.

"Then how do you explain her blood test results?" Doug asked.

Cassidy's shoulders sagged. "I can't. Unless someone made a mistake."

Kyle cringed. "Oh, the lab rats would love to hear that."

"Lab rats?" Now *she* was confused.

"The county lab assistants. Dr. Melanie Hutton-Cooper, the local coroner/forensic anthropologist, and our buddy Jason's wife, tagged them with the moniker, and the rest of us have latched on to it."

Wow, the Anderson County Sheriff's Department really had a close relationship. She couldn't wrap her mind around the easygoing nature of the group. Sure, she enjoyed the people she worked with and even went out with on occasion, but ACSD took it to a whole new level. She better be careful with what she said, or Kyle might add another reason not to like her. "I'd hate to hurt their feelings, but if they didn't mess up, who did?"

Doug shifted to face her and raised a brow.

"Look. I know that you think I'm making something out of nothing. But I'm telling you, it's impossible. Laura didn't drink. And if by the slim chance she did, and I do mean slim, she *never* would have driven."

Kyle rubbed the back of his neck. "Let's not argue the point. We'll take another look at the case file and have Mel reexamine the autopsy report."

Cassidy blinked back tears, threatening to fall. "Thank you."

Doug tapped the map. "There is something about these. They're too clustered to be random. Although, not impossible."

She held her breath that Kyle and Doug would agree with her enough to convince the sheriff to dig a little deeper.

Kyle pinched his lips together and huffed. "I concur with my partner. I'm not on board with your theory. But I'm willing to take it a step further. I say we pull in the others. If we all take a few interviews, we can compare notes and decide whether or not to pursue the serial killer idea." He pulled the cell phone from his pocket, turned his back to her and strode to the front window.

Her lungs deflated in relief.

She would've continued her search for the truth with or without the ACSD, but the recent target on her back changed things. Cassidy desperately wanted someone to believe her. Her life was at stake, and Laura deserved to have her killer behind bars.

The fact that Kyle hadn't refused to consider her premise a possibility almost took her to her knees.

Phone to his ear, Kyle slipped his fingers between the slats of the blinds and nudged them open. He peered out, searching for anything out of the ordinary. Had the man who'd tried to kill Cassidy followed them to Doug's?

Deep down, he knew that he and Doug hadn't led the maniac to the house, but uncertainty had raised its ugly head. He couldn't—wouldn't—deny that Cassidy had stumbled onto something odd. But a serial killer? That, he doubted. But he felt as if he owed her for his bad behavior. And if they gave her a day or two of their time, what would it hurt?

"Sheriff Monroe." Dennis's voice rang out over the line.

"Hey, boss." Kyle dropped the slats. "We have a recommendation."

"That didn't take long." Dennis paused. "Should I be worried about what to tell Cassidy's supervisor?"

"Worried, no. Cautious about what she's found, yes." He ran a hand over his face. "Doug and I both agree that her concern has merit."

Silence lingered long enough that Kyle checked his phone to make sure that Dennis hadn't hung up.

"I'm not sure what I expected to hear you say, but I'm a bit surprised you think it's possible there's a serial killer on the loose. Is the evidence that overwhelming?"

"Not at all. In fact, it's very underwhelming."

"Detective Howard, I think you better explain yourself if I'm putting manpower into this."

Uh-oh, Dennis had shifted to serious. "Let's just say Doug and I both have a hinky feeling about the cases Cassidy tagged. We aren't suggesting it's the work of a serial killer…" Kyle looked over his shoulder and caught Cassidy staring at him. "But we can't deny someone's out to kill her."

"No. We can't look past that. Hold on." Muffled voices grew in volume, and dogs barked in the background. "Sorry about that. I just walked in the door, and my greeting party came running."

"Not a problem." He loved Dennis's sudden family. His boss had had a quiet life until about a year ago when his five-year-old daughter landed on his doorstep. Then several months later, he and Charlotte met while shutting down an adoption ring that led them to Charlotte's daughter, who she thought had died as an infant, adding to the chaos and throwing the poor man for a loop. But the precious girls and their two dogs were a riot to be around.

"I'm not saying we agree with her. I think the attacks on Cassidy are more than likely someone from her past that she put behind bars. Or a family member of a convicted felon." Kyle rubbed the back of his neck. "Dennis... I don't know what to think. I'm skeptical."

"That's what makes you a good detective."

The praise meant a lot to Kyle, and he didn't want to lose his boss's trust. "I guess what I'm trying to say is I'd like to give her the benefit of the doubt."

"Is this because of Amber and how you left things with Cassidy?"

"Maybe." His guilt played a part in his willingness to look into her cases. "Probably."

A deep sigh filtered over the line. Dennis's sign of intense thought. "All right then, I'll go with your recommendation—for now. What do you need from the rest of us?"

"I'd like everyone to take a few families and friends of the deceased and interview them again with an open mind and not a preconceived conclusion."

"Email everyone their assignment. Y'all can start tomorrow. I'll clear the way with the head of each department and let them know that we're following up on a possible connection to another case. I won't say anything about a serial killer, just that we're working on a theory. You have a couple days, but I can't ignore our other responsibilities for longer than that unless we find something definitive."

"Sounds fair." Beyond fair if you asked Kyle, and he appreciated it. "Thanks, Dennis."

"I'd say anytime, but I wouldn't mean it." Dennis laughed. Little girls' squeals of delight sounded in the background. "Gotta go." His boss hung up.

Kyle tapped his phone on his palm. His boss and friend sounded happy. Not that the man hadn't been content before—they all envied the easygoing sheriff's ability to set aside stress and appreciate life—but Charlotte and the girls added a layer of joy to the man.

Kyle's grandparents had raised him after his parents died in a car accident on Christmas Eve. Nana and Pops had that kind of relationship. One filled with joy and contentment. Not that they didn't argue, but the love flowed around them. Pops had died a couple of years ago, and since then, Nana's health had declined. He'd always wanted what his grandparents had.

God, why did Amber have to die? I wanted to spend the rest of my life with her. Have a family and grow old together.

Nana's biggest longing was for him to settle down. Maybe give her a great-grandchild for her to dote on. She didn't have many years left, and the woman of his dreams was gone.

"Kyle, is everything okay?"

He straightened and pulled in a breath. Cassidy had stepped next to him, and he hadn't noticed. "Dennis is giving us two days to interview the families and find solid proof of your suspicions."

"That's great. Let's get to it." The smile on her lips did weird things to his insides. Things he shouldn't feel for many reasons.

He wanted to give in to her plow-forward attitude, but common sense reigned. He tamped down the direction his mind had gone and remembered why he'd walked away from their friendship before he did something stupid.

"Not tonight. We'll head out tomorrow." She started to interrupt, but he held up his hand. "I'm divvying up the list with the others, and the sheriff needs time to contact the departments. We don't barge into other jurisdictions without them knowing. Tomorrow is soon enough. Amongst all of us, we'll cover a lot of ground. But tonight, we need to make a plan and get some sleep."

Cassidy touched the bruises on her neck and stared at the floor. "You're right. I'm thankful you're willing to work with me."

Years of friendship had him wanting to pull her into a hug, but he refrained, not ready to put his pain aside. He had to blame someone for Amber's death, and Cassidy fell into that role.

Yet, she deserved better from him. What was that old saying? Was he a man or a mouse? More like a rat. His final words to Amber rattled around in his brain. If only he could take them back.

He shook off the thoughts and sighed. "I know the past is a huge boulder between us, but I'm not an ogre. I don't want anything to happen to you. And if you're right about the killer, we have to stop him."

She met his gaze and nodded.

"Come on. I want to get the information to Doug and my counterparts, Jason and Keith, then we'll make dinner and get some rest."

Without a word, Cassidy rejoined Doug and grabbed a pad of paper. "If everyone takes an area, it'll cut down on time." She raised her pen and pointed to the map. "Focus on these four clusters and not the outliers, except for my cousin Laura's case. We'll deal with them later. I'm confident you'll discover they are all homicides and a connection between them."

Kyle wasn't as sure about the results, but he and his co-workers would do a thorough job.

"I agree with your plan." He grabbed the laptop and typed the email, assigning each detective a location and attached the files for each victim. He cc'd Dennis, then closed the computer. "Done. Cassidy, why don't you go take a shower and get comfortable for the evening?"

"Are you sure? I'd be happy to help." She waved a hand at the coffee table.

He shook his head. The woman looked ready to drop. But that was Cassidy. Push through and get the job done. "Go. Relax. Enjoy a long hot shower."

"Thanks." Cassidy ambled down the hallway and out of sight.

Doug pointed to the scattered files and photos. "I'll go fix dinner while you straighten up in here."

Kyle almost laughed at his partner. Doug's OCD tendencies were showing. He was surprised the man had lasted that long without tidying up. Come to think of it, it shocked him that Cassidy hadn't spent time organizing the documents like she had when they'd started. In all the time he'd known her, she had similar obsessive-compulsive behaviors that rivaled Doug's.

He took pity on Doug and made quick work of stacking the documents and organizing the coffee table, then strode to the kitchen to help his partner with the food prep.

"What is with you? I can feel the tension flowing off you." Doug stood at the stove, stirring the spaghetti sauce.

"I…" He contemplated how to answer as he pulled lettuce from the refrigerator and chopped it for a salad. He didn't hate her. It was more like he hated being around her and the guilt she produced in him. That was more accurate. "She reminds me of what I lost. And I blame her for not being more careful."

He'd never admitted to anyone that his words to Amber before her shift had likely caused her death. Just like his final words to his parents before they had died. But if Cassidy had watched out for Amber…

"Hmm. So, I suppose you'd blame me for my wife's death."

Kyle spun to face him. "No way."

"But I wasn't here to protect her. I'm a security specialist and should've had my home better prepared." Doug stared him down.

"You couldn't have known. None of that was your fault." Kyle wanted to shake the man. He couldn't have stopped what happened while overseas serving his country. And from what Kyle read in the report, Doug's wife had a target on her no matter where it happened.

"Exactly. Don't get me wrong, sometimes the guilt creeps in. I'm her husband. I should have protected her. But I know the blame doesn't lie with me." Doug returned his attention to the pot on the stove and turned off the burner. "I've just met Cassidy, but I can tell she's a good cop. She wouldn't have endangered her partner—her friend—if she'd known about the explosive."

Doug had him there. "I'll think about it."

Doug slapped him on the back on his way to grab plates from the cupboard. "That's all I ask." He placed the last item on the table and gripped the back of a chair. "You aren't telling the whole story."

Kyle about dropped the pitcher of tea he held. "What are you talking about?"

"Come on, man. There's more to Amber's death than you're saying." Doug pursed his lips. "You can keep your secret for now. But sooner or later, you'll have to spill it."

How had his partner come to that conclusion? Either way, Doug had called him on it. "I'm not sure what to say."

Doug waved him off. "That's a discussion for another time."

To disclose his horrible words to Amber that morning meant admitting guilt over her death. Should he tell Doug?

"That smells good." Cassidy entered the kitchen, decked out in comfy sweats, and her hair in a messy bun.

The sight brought back memories of him, Amber and her hanging out on the weekends, watching movies and relaxing after a long work week. A lump lodged in his throat.

"Hope you like it." Doug motioned for Cassidy to sit.

Kyle shrugged off the memory and joined them at the table, choosing the seat across from Cassidy instead of beside her. "Doug's a great cook, and the sauce is his recipe."

"Wow, I'm impressed." Cassidy filled her plate.

Doug handed her the bowl of shredded cheese. "Don't be. My mother refused to let her boys leave home without knowing how to cook and do laundry."

"Smart woman." Kyle twisted the spaghetti around his fork. Not for the first time, his heart ached at the loss of his parents. At least he had his Pops and Nana, but Pops was gone, and with Nana's failing memory and age, he had limited time with her.

After the small group's pleasant dinner and cleaning the kitchen, Cassidy excused herself and headed to her room. He and Doug checked the doors, windows and security system. Deeming everything safe, they headed to bed.

Several hours later, Kyle lay on his back and stared at the ceiling, unable to shut off his mind. Cassidy's sudden appearance had thrown him for a loop. Wanting to protect her and holding on to his bitterness fought against each other, making his brain hurt. Not to mention his heart and his own guilt.

He missed Amber, but so did Cassidy. All he had to do was look into her eyes to see the depth of grief. The three of them had once been good friends and spent hours together.

When he'd walked away from her, he hadn't realized how much he'd feel that loss as well. He flipped over and punched his pillow to get more comfortable. He flopped back down and sighed. His thoughts had tangled his belly into a knot. So much for sleep tonight.

The security alarm blared, jolting Kyle from his bed.

He snatched the Glock from the nightstand and raced out of the bedroom. He came inches from running into Doug in the hall. The two of them rushed to the living room.

A figure stood at the front door.

Kyle raised his weapon. "Police! Don't move!" he yelled over the ear-piercing sound.

The person spun and pointed a gun at him.

Finger on the trigger, he fought the instinct to pull. He blinked. "Cassidy?" Kyle brought his weapon down.

"I've got it." Doug punched in the code to shut off the alarm, made a quick call to cancel the emergency request with the security company and rejoined them.

"Where are you going?" Kyle slid the Glock into the waistband of his sweatpants.

Confusion crossed her features. She lowered her Glock next to her leg. "Nowhere. I couldn't sleep, so I came out to get a cup of tea. The alarm went off, and I ran to look out the window for an intruder. Then you showed up a moment later."

"You didn't set off the security system?" The muscles in Kyle's neck tensed.

She shook her head. "No."

His gaze darted to Doug.

"On it." His partner jogged down the hall to his office.

"Get away from the window." Kyle pulled Cassidy to the couch and hurried to the kitchen. He flipped off the stove that heated the teakettle and turned off the light above the sink, plunging the house into darkness.

"Kyle." Doug's tone worried him.

He strode to join his partner, who stood in the living

room, laptop in one hand while he tapped furiously with the other.

"What did you find?"

"Someone was out there."

"Doug." Kyle yanked his 9 mm from his waistband.

His partner stepped next to Cassidy. "I've got her. Go!"

Kyle sprinted out the back door and locked it behind him. He tucked in next to the house, letting his eyesight adjust to the darkness.

The moonlight reflected off the icy grass. He hurried to the trees that lined the perimeter and plastered himself to the trunk of an old oak. Movement to his left had him halt his plans. Limbs cracked, and dry leaves crunched, indicating the prowler headed toward the main street. He ducked low and wove his way toward the sound, Glock held next to his leg.

An engine started, and tires squealed.

Kyle broke through the bushes near the driveway in time to see taillights disappear around the corner.

He leaned forward and placed his hands on his knees. The cold air made goose bumps appear on his arms. His breath turned white and swirled in the air.

Frustration weighed down on him. Twice, he'd come close to catching Cassidy's attacker. And twice, he'd failed.

He hung his head and dragged himself to the house. With a quick rap on the door, he called out, "It's Kyle. Open up."

Doug greeted him with the barrel of his gun. When his partner confirmed it was Kyle, he lowered his weapon. "Anything?"

"Yeah, but he got away." He laid his Glock on the coffee table within reach in case the intruder returned.

Doug motioned him to the laptop and tapped the screen.

Kyle's stomach dropped to the floor.

"What is it?" Cassidy asked.

How did he tell her that someone had almost gotten in? He shook his head.

Cassidy stood and crossed her arms. "If it's nothing, then why are you two treating this like someone plans to burn the place down?"

Before Kyle responded, Doug spoke up. "We can't tell who, but the person wore baggy clothes and had a hand on the doorknob. From the video, he looks like a home-less man."

"As in, he tried to break in?" She ran her fingers through her hair.

Kyle's feet had a mind of their own, and he found him-self standing in front of her.

"With everything going on, I should have been more careful checking the window." Her pallor worried him.

"We're here to help. I wish I could've caught him." Guilt gnawed at him for not protecting Cassidy better.

Her shoulders wilted. "You did your best. Thank you for chasing after him." The light from outside seeped through the small slits in the blinds, giving him a view of the slight smile that graced her face.

He turned his attention to Doug to avoid doing some-thing stupid like pulling her into his arms to comfort her. "Or is this just a random person looking for something to steal? I'm not sure I buy the homeless angle. The dude had a car. I guess it's possible he's living out of it. Bottom line, did the attacker find her?"

"Good question. I'll print out stills and send the video to the county lab for analysis." Doug sat and took care of busi-ness, then closed the laptop. "I'm not one for coincidences. I think it's a good idea if we take turns standing guard."

"I'll take the first watch. Relieve me in a few hours."

Kyle's need to protect her surfaced, and he didn't fight it. Besides, he wouldn't fall asleep anytime soon.

Doug nodded and left him alone with Cassidy.

Kyle brushed her arm with his hand. "Go on. Get some sleep."

"I feel stupid. I'm a detective for the love of everything. I shouldn't need a bodyguard. And I should have taken the security alert more seriously. I don't know what's gotten into me. I'm better than that," Cassidy huffed.

"Cass." Without thinking, her old nickname rolled off his tongue. "Sometimes, we don't want to believe the reality of what we're going through, so we ignore the warning signs. It's a natural reaction. And everyone needs help from time to time. Just ask the guys I work with. Even if we haven't decided we are on board with your serial killer theory, we know you need protection. And we take that seriously."

"Thank you for that." Had the woman with the tough exterior sniffed like she was crying? "I'll go on to bed then. Let me know if I can help."

"Will do." Kyle watched her move down the hall through the dark house.

Once Cassidy disappeared out of sight, he plopped on the couch and dropped his face into his hands. The push-pull of emotions toward Cassidy gave him a headache.

"God, I need to know exactly what happened with Amber, but I'm afraid to ask," he whispered.

Had his words ultimately caused her death?

FIVE

The snow-covered scenery added an icy sparkle to the Christmas decorations adorning the streets. One, most years, Cassidy would enjoy. But this year—today— sitting in Kyle's truck while on the way to the first interview, her mood sank. The hope and joy that Christmas normally filled her with had gone dormant. She was unsure if she'd ever approach the holiday with love again. Is this what Kyle experienced for all those years before he met Amber? How had he lived with the despair?

The drive gave her too much time to think. Cassidy had slept last night, but not much. Her mind kept whirling. What had she done to attract the attention of the serial killer? Each case filtered through her mind. Who had she talked to? What evidence had she uncovered? Then when she'd drifted off, Kyle's kindness filled her dreams. Her uncharacteristic reaction to his touch when he'd grounded her in the living room baffled her. What did she do with that?

The puzzle pieces of the cases, not to mention her feelings for Kyle, refused to fit together. She rubbed her temples.

"Doing okay?" Kyle asked, tugging her from her musing.

She shifted to look at him, unsure how to answer his question.

He brushed a wave of his black hair off his forehead,

and the dimples in his cheeks deepened with his sympathetic smile.

Cassidy couldn't deny the man had a strength about
him. And handsome? Oh, yes. Handsome indeed.

She almost laughed out loud at her wayward thoughts.
The fatigue must be greater than she thought. "I'm good.
Just thinking."

"About?"

Why am I thinking about you so much? But she wouldn't
say that. "What I did to become the focus of a killer." He
seemed to be able to read her expression, so she might as
well be honest with him. "I wish I knew what I discovered
that caused it."

"If your theory's correct—which I'm not saying that it
is, but *if* you are right—my guess is that you got too close
to the truth. Maybe even talked to him."

She shivered. Had she come face-to-face with the killer?

He leaned forward and adjusted the temperature. "When
do you think this guy started following you?"

Cassidy wanted to tell him her reaction had nothing to
do with the temperature, but instead, she shrugged. "I don't
know." She reached back into the recesses of her mind.
When was the first time she'd felt his presence? She tapped
her bottom lip. "Definitely the day of the fire."

"That's a given." Kyle kept his eyes on the road, but a
slight upward curve formed on his mouth. Almost like he
wanted to continue to tease her but held back.

In all the times she'd spent with the man when he came
over to visit Amber, his fun-loving side had taken the fore-
front. But now…a more serious version of him sat beside
her. Had Amber's death caused him to shy away from
living? Since he'd walked away from Cassidy, she had no
idea what his life had consisted of for the last nine months.

She returned her gaze to the passing landscape. Guilt

pressed in. She should have stowed her hurt and reached out to him. Demanded that he talk with her. But he wanted the details of the raid. Cassidy couldn't give him that. Or wouldn't. She hadn't allowed herself to force the memory. Her brain had chosen to protect itself and had forgotten those final moments. The physical pain, too great. The emotional—she refused to go there.

By the time she'd recovered enough to leave the hospital, he'd already walked away. His cold shoulder had stung, but she'd had her own issues to deal with, so she'd let him go.

Awkward didn't begin to describe the silence that engulfed the cab of the truck for the rest of the drive.

He parked in front of an apartment building and shut off the engine. "This is where Hannah Perkins lives. Her son Aaron was presumed drowned while out on the lake." Kyle grabbed the file from the seat and flipped through the pages. "According to the report, Aaron, age thirty, had gone boating alone. Because of a mixture of blood and hair on the rail, they suspect he fell, hit his head and went overboard. However, even after a lengthy search, they never found his body."

"I remember this case." Cassidy straightened, refocusing on the task at hand. "His mom refused to believe it and said he always wore his life jacket and would never have gone out alone on a boat without it."

"There's always a first time, especially if alcohol or drugs are involved. And we can't rule out suicide." Kyle opened his door and stepped out.

She joined him at the front of the vehicle. "Or not. Granted, those angles are inconclusive, and without a body, we'll never know for sure. I called the mom to clarify the notes the officer had made, and she told me that when Aaron was five, his little brother, a toddler at the time, had drowned. The child wandered off during a family camping trip. They found him an hour later, facedown in the lake. It affected Aaron, and for a long time, he refused to go near large bodies of water. But over the years, he faced his fears and returned to the activity he always loved, but he never went boating without a life jacket. Determined that his mother wouldn't lose another child like that. Like Laura, he never would have taken the chance because of what happened in his past."

Kyle released a heavy sigh. "When you put it like that… Let's go see what Ms. Perkins has to say."

Cold air swirled, kicking up dried leaves around Cassidy's shoes. She zipped up her jacket and pulled the edges tighter. "It got chilly all of a sudden."

"Looks like the weather is turning, and we might get a white Christmas after all." He strode next to her up the walkway.

Christmas. She sighed, remembering how she and Amber decorated their little apartment to the point of too much. They'd collapse on the couch and laugh at how overboard they'd gone. And on Christmas Eve, she and Amber went to church and absorbed the peacefulness of the season, and thanked God for all He'd done. She missed her friend this year and the joy they shared. Her faith had plummeted. Could she muster up the courage to step foot in the church on Christmas Eve with all the memories crashing down?

He stopped at the entrance and knocked.

The door opened. A woman with gray streaks in her shoulder-length hair stood at the entrance. "May I help you?"

Kyle glanced at Cassidy, raised a brow and took the lead when she didn't respond.

"Ms. Perkins, I'm Detective Kyle Howard, and this is Detective Cassidy Bowman."

The lady smiled. "Oh yes, I remember Ms. Bowman. Nice to see you again."

"You as well." Cassidy inhaled, not wanting to cause the mother any more pain. "I hate to bother you, but we have a few questions about your son Aaron. Detective Howard would like to hear your answers firsthand if you don't mind."

Ms. Perkins held open the door and motioned them inside. "Since you're the only one willing to listen to my concerns, I'm more than happy to talk with you."

"Thank you for your time." Kyle sat on one end of the couch, and Cassidy sat on the other.

Ms. Perkins drilled Kyle with a glare. "Are you going to toe the company line and say my son had an accident, or are you willing to hear out an old lady and listen to reason?"

Wide-eyed, Kyle stared at the woman. "I…uh—"

"Not much for words, are you?"

Cassidy coughed to cover her laugh. She'd forgotten to mention Ms. Perkins's feisty side.

"No, ma'am. I mean, yes, ma'am."

"Well, which is it, son?"

Kyle held up a hand. "I'm here to listen to what you have to say. Then I'll form my opinion without bias."

Cassidy watched the silent standoff between Kyle and Ms. Perkins. Taking pity on Kyle, she leaned forward. "Great. Let's go over what you told me."

Ms. Perkins nodded. "You see, my boy Aaron always loved the water. But after his baby brother drowned during a family outing—" Hannah blinked back tears. "At first, he was afraid of the water, but as he grew older, he worked through his fears and returned to what he'd always loved. Boating and fishing with his father. But he became obsessed with water safety. At one point, after my husband passed away from a heart attack while Aaron was in college, I thought he might sell the boat. Too many losses in his young life. But he loved boating too much to walk away. But that didn't mean his safety-conscious self went away. He refused to let anyone on his boat without a life jacket."

"I'm sure his little brother's death was hard on him." Cassidy knew the feeling. The extra safeguards. The vigilance. She and Laura had experienced the whole gamut of emotions and responses.

"Oh, it was, dear. At one point, it was like an obsession. But we found him a wonderful counselor that helped him work through that. Years later, he still demanded the precautions, but the obsession faded."

"Was he still seeing his therapist?" Kyle rested his arms on his knees.

Ms. Perkins glared at him. "I know what you're implying. But to answer your question, yes. He had a standing appointment once a month. His choice. Not hers."

"We have to look at where the evidence takes us and cover all possibilities."

Ms. Perkins harrumphed.

"Hannah, please understand that Detective Howard is just doing his job."

The woman crossed her arms.

So much for defusing the situation.

"What did the officers say about your theory?" Kyle asked.

"It wasn't a theory." Ms. Perkins pointed a finger at Kyle. "My Aaron didn't have an accident. Someone killed him. Go ask his longtime friend Robert Hansen. He and Aaron took the boat out fishing the day before. Robert will tell you the same things I have about Aaron's habits."

Cassidy jotted down Robert's name. She hadn't remembered hearing about him before. Once she returned to the truck, she'd look up an address and phone number.

The crease in Kyle's forehead deepened. "I can see why you disagree with the results of the police report."

Ms. Perkins stood. "Now that you understand why the police got it wrong, I want you to go find who did it."

"Yes, ma'am." Kyle pushed to his feet, shook the older woman's hand and headed for the front door.

Cassidy hung back a moment. "Thank you, Ms. Perkins."

"Honey, I'm the one who should thank you. If not for your insistence, no one would have taken a second look at Aaron's death. Even if Mr. Serious isn't so sure."

She attempted to hide her smile at Hannah's description of Kyle but failed. Cassidy hugged the older woman and whispered in her ear. "I think you scared him."

The lady chuckled. "He needed a kick in the pants."

Cassidy shoved her hands in her coat pockets and stepped onto the sidewalk. "Thank you again for talking with us."

"I'm glad to do it, sweetie. Especially if you can find my son's killer."

"The sheriff's department might not agree with me, but I don't plan on letting it go until I find answers." She waved at Hannah, then followed Kyle to the truck and climbed in. "I told you."

Kyle still had a dazed look from his whirlwind experience named Ms. Perkins. "Okay. Okay. I'm starting to see your point."

Cassidy patted his arm. "See. Was that so hard?"

"What are you talking about?" He turned his attention to her.

"Saying that I'm right." She gave him her best cheesy grin.

"I never said…" He shook his head. "Don't mess with me like that."

"Why on Earth not? It's so much fun." She held her breath, praying he'd loosen up. The old Kyle had peeked through, and she couldn't resist the tease.

He rolled his eyes, but the struggle to keep the smirk off his face was evident. His fingers drummed on the steering wheel. He threw a glance her way. "You enjoyed seeing me struggle with Ms. Perkins, didn't you."

"I—" She smiled.

The banter between them felt like old times. Too bad they couldn't return there.

"That's what I thought." Kyle cranked the engine. Cassidy's playfulness had him off balance. His determination to hold her at arm's length had failed on multiple occasions. When they worked together, the old friendship had sneaked in.

"I want to talk with his counselor and explore the depression angle."

Cassidy buckled her seat belt. "I don't think he took his own life."

"Maybe. Maybe not. But as you said, I wouldn't be doing my job if I didn't consider it."

Cassidy nodded. "I'll get the name and number of Aaron's therapist for you."

"Thank you. Now, who's next?"

Cassidy tapped her cell phone. "I want to talk to Robert Hansen. Hannah didn't mention him before. From what I know from my investigation, this information tells us that Hansen was the last to see Aaron alive."

Kyle swung his gaze to her. "You think he killed Aaron Perkins?"

"I did *not* say that. Robert Hansen's name is not in the report. He has knowledge of the state of Mr. Perkin's boat and his emotional state. He might know if Aaron's boat had mechanical problems or if the man was worried or acting off."

"I agree. I find it weird that there is no mention of him before today."

"I'm curious about that as well. I wonder if she mentioned Hansen to the police and it never made it into the report."

"Not a clue." Kyle stared at Ms. Perkins's house. Cassidy's kindness, standing up for him about doing his job—she didn't have to do that. He'd planned to stay with the basics to get a handle on the case. They were, after all, on a fishing expedition for information. Not doing a full investigation.

"Kyle?"

He glanced at her. "What did you say?"

"I asked if you're ready to go."

"Yeah. Sorry about that." He put the truck into gear. He'd better get his head in the game before Cassidy decided to ditch him for a more focused detective.

"I hope Hansen can give us something to work with. Let's try to catch him at work." She returned her attention to her phone and rattled off the address.

Kyle went one further. He hoped the team got enough information to either confirm or reject Cassidy's serial killer theory. He hated living in limbo. Of course, that described his last nine months. Living, but without direction.

The truck cab remained silent while Cassidy scrolled on her phone, pulling up data and jotting things in the margins of the copy of Aaron's report.

Twenty-five minutes later, Kyle pulled into 4Gen Tech's lot and parked next to a two-story building. "Nice place."

"Says here that Robert worked for a tech company called Quick Fox Technology until the owner, Lewis Fox, dismissed him a few years ago. Now he works for John Morrison, the witness to a carjacking, and our next interview. Robert's been employed there for the past year."

"That's interesting. Wonder what the connection is." Kyle exited the truck and strode up the walkway. Cassidy stayed in step with him. When they reached the door, he held it open for her.

The interior of 4Gen Tech reminded him of a high-class hotel. Morrison had done well for himself.

A woman with long blond hair in black slacks and a blue blouse greeted them. Khloe Trammell, according to the nameplate on the desk. "May I help you?"

Kyle held up his badge. "Detective Howard and my colleague, Detective Bowman. We're here to see Robert Hansen."

The woman frowned. "Is something wrong?"

"No, ma'am. Everything is fine. We'd like to ask Mr. Hansen a few questions about his friend Aaron Perkins."

Khloe's hand went to her chest. "What a terrible accident. We were all devastated."

"Yes, ma'am, I'm sure." Kyle blinked. "Wait. You knew Mr. Perkins?"

"Oh yes. Aaron was a pillar of the company."

He shifted his gaze to Cassidy, who appeared as confused as him.

Cassidy recovered from the unexpected information. "Is Mr. Hansen available? We really need to talk with him."

"Unfortunately, he traveled to Stonebridge and won't be in until tomorrow."

"What about Mr. Morrison?"

"I'm sorry, but he worked from home today." The phone rang. Khloe placed her hand on the receiver, prepared to pick it up. "If you'll excuse me, I need to get back to work."

Kyle removed a business card from his wallet and handed it to the woman. "Please ask Robert to give me a call when he has a moment. It's important that I talk with him."

"Sure. I'll let him know right away." Khloe placed the card on the desk and answered the phone. "4Gen Tech, how may I help you?"

Kyle gestured toward the door, and Cassidy led the way outside.

"Well, that didn't go as planned." She sighed.

They returned to the truck. He drummed his fingers on the steering wheel. "Mr. Morrison is next on the list?"

Cassidy nodded and gave him the man's home address.

"What do we know about him?"

She opened the file. "John Morrison. Apparently, he knows our drowning victim, but in addition, he was the first on the shooting scene of our victims, Sandy and Michael Hughes. Later, he became the target of a hit-and-run."

"The guy's connected in multiple ways. It might be nothing, but it is interesting. What happened with the hit-and-run?"

Cassidy flipped through the report. "It says he had non-life-threatening injuries. Major bruising, but nothing broken. I'd say he's fortunate it didn't do more damage."

Kyle left the business district and headed to Mr. Morrison's house. "Did he have any specifics on the suspect from the shooting or his incident?"

She glanced down at the document. "Nothing more than a basic description of the suspect. White male, average height and weight, thirty to forty, dark hair. Baggy clothes. Maybe homeless. Nothing stood out except for his unkempt appearance. Could be anybody." She tapped her chin. "What's up with a homeless man showing up at all these scenes?"

"Does seem strange, doesn't it." The description worried him. It matched the same person at Doug's door last night. If Cassidy had made the connection to the lurker, she didn't say anything. Mental note to self, mention his suspicions to Doug.

The lack of solid information bothered him. "Generic description. That's what I was afraid of. What about the hit-and-run?"

"He had his back turned to the car, and there were no witnesses."

Kyle exhaled. "Figures. Let's not forget to ask him about Aaron Perkins as well."

The tires hummed on the pavement. Kyle took a right, maneuvered through a middle-class neighborhood, flashed his badge at the security officer and entered a gated community.

Cassidy straightened and took in the houses that dotted both sides of the street. Not what she'd expected. "I don't think these people hurt for money."

He leaned forward and peered through the windshield. "I guess not. What do you think? A mill, maybe two?"

"That would be my guess." These home prices in the small midwestern town of Valley Springs spoke of money and lots of it.

"Here we are." Kyle pulled up to a sizable Mediterranean-style home. Complete with a circular drive.

He whistled through his teeth. "Wow! How much does his company make?"

"I read he partnered with his friends and built a software business from the ground up. Although, I never found the names of his original business partners." Cassidy dropped from the truck, still staring at the house. "I hope we're dressed appropriately."

"Yeah, too bad that my tux is at the cleaners. Come on." Kyle strode to the door and rang the bell.

She hurried to catch up and stood next to him while they waited for someone to answer.

The door opened, and a man in his forties greeted them. "Good morning. May I help you?"

"I'm Detective Kyle Howard, and this is Detective Cassidy Bowman. We're here to speak with Mr. Morrison. I called earlier about stopping by."

"That would be me," the man said.

"Nice to meet you." Kyle shook the man's hand. "We'd like to ask you a few more questions about the crime you witnessed, and the hit-and-run." He had no intention of bringing up Aaron. At least not yet.

"Certainly. Come in." He motioned them inside. "I'm not sure what I can add. That happened—what—a year ago?"

"Something like that." Cassidy knew the cases had passed the year mark.

Kyle caught her quick glance at him. How would the man not remember how long ago someone tried to run him over? If it were him, an incident like that would be burned in Kyle's brain. The man's demeanor had an oddness to it that he couldn't put his finger on.

Mr. Morrison escorted them to the living room. When they'd sat, he offered them beverages, which they declined.

Cassidy took the lead. "I've read the report, but I'd like to hear your statement about the shooting from you."

"I know they never found the guy. Are you reopening the case? Do you have any leads?"

"We're not at liberty to divulge that information. But hearing the details again might help us answer a few questions that have come to our attention," Cassidy said.

Mr. Morrison rested his elbows on his knees and stared at the floor.

Kyle's gaze landed on her. He arched his brow and mouthed, *Not at liberty to say?*

She choked back the laugh. Cassidy made a funny face at him and shrugged.

Kyle pinched his lips in a line and cleared his throat. "I'd like to hear your statement firsthand. Anything you can tell us would be great." If the team decided Cassidy's theory warranted a full investigation, he'd return and properly question Mr. Morrison. Until then, he'd simply listen and look for inconsistencies.

When Mr. Morrison finished his account of what he'd witnessed, Kyle could tell Cassidy wanted to throw something. The man had given the same account with nothing new to add. Although, the words bothered him. Too similar to the original statement for Kyle's liking, as if he'd memorized it.

"Could you tell us about the hit-and-run?" Kyle asked.

"Not much to say. I was out for a run. The car came from behind. I heard the engine rev and looked over my shoulder. The car sped up, aiming straight for me. I dove out of the way and tumbled down a small embankment. As a result, I sported scrapes and bruises for weeks."

"Any information you can give us on the make and model of the car? Maybe the license plate number?"

John shook his head. "A dark-colored car is all I remember."

"I'm sorry we had to bring up all the bad memories again." Cassidy's gentle tone had Kyle feeling sympathy for the man—almost.

"I do have one more question. What can you tell me about Aaron Perkins?" He studied John Morrison's reaction.

Mr. Morrison winced at the name. Subtle, but Kyle noticed. A quick look at Cassidy told him she'd seen the response too.

"He was a college friend and a great businessman. His accident shocked the whole company."

"When did you see him last before he died?" Cassidy asked.

"I traveled that week, so probably four or five days."

"Honey." A woman in a tan dress and heels and without a blond hair out of place entered the room. "I apologize for the interruption, but you have a phone call."

"Thank you, Caroline." Mr. Morrison stood. "If you'll excuse me. Caroline will answer any other questions you might have, but I need to take this call."

Cassidy and Kyle stood.

Mr. Morrison left the room, and Caroline joined them. "Is there anything else I can do for you?"

Cassidy ambled to the pictures on the mantel.

Kyle wanted time to ponder the entire conversation and explore the information John had given them. "I think we have everything we need. But we'll let you know if we think of anything else." Like why John reacted to Aaron's name. And confirming he was out of town before his friend's death. Kyle paused. "Cassidy?"

She turned to face Caroline. "I find this picture fascinating. Are these the friends your husband started his business with?"

Mrs. Morrison walked over and ran a finger over the frame. "Yes. That was ages ago. They were all very close."

Cassidy faced Mrs. Morrison. "Thank you again for your time."

"We are glad to help our local law enforcement." Caroline escorted them to the door and held it open.

After a final goodbye, they left and headed out of the neighborhood.

"Want to grab lunch before we interview another family?" Kyle asked.

"Sounds good to me. I'm starved." Cassidy's brow furrowed as she stared at the trees going by.

She'd become distant at the end of the interview. He'd give almost anything to know what was going on in that mind of hers.

"You're awfully quiet. Anything I should know?" Kyle aimed the truck toward downtown.

"I'm not sure. Let me noodle it a while." She turned her

attention to him. "We've gotten along pretty well today, and I don't want to ruin that…"

He exhaled. "But?"

"We really need to talk."

So much for brushing the past aside while they worked together. Kyle's grip tightened on the steering wheel. "About what?"

A humorless laugh fell from her lips. "I think you know."

Yeah, he did. The raid and what happened. But he had no desire to go there. Not knowing what to say, he simply nodded.

A few moments later, he parked at the cozy café, one of his favorite eating establishments in Valley Springs.

The street lights sported red, green and gold tinsel, candles, wreaths and holly. A community Christmas tree sat in the park near the main street that defined downtown. The store owners had rigged up a speaker system, and Christmas music filled the air.

The joyous atmosphere amplified his loss. Would he ever enjoy the holiday season again?

He led Cassidy to the café. They made their way inside and took a seat at a booth in the back.

Their waitress, Sally, placed glasses of water and menus, along with Kyle's typical cup of coffee, in front of them and strode off to help another customer.

Cassidy opened her menu. "What's good?"

"Everything."

She leveled him with a glare.

He chuckled. "I'm being serious. Although, if you don't want to deal with heartburn, stay away from the chili cheese fries."

"Good to know."

Sally returned, took their orders and left them alone.

Too bad. Kyle wasn't ready for the coming conversation. In fact, he wanted to skip it altogether.

Cassidy took a sip and returned her glass to the table. She wiped the droplets that had fallen, then folded her hands and released a heavy sigh.

Oh boy, here it comes.

"I'm sorry you lost Amber. I know how much you loved her." Cassidy's words hit him square in the chest.

Air refused to fill his lungs. He hadn't expected her to be so blunt. Nor did he expect any form of an apology. "I— Thank you." He traced his thumb along the rim of his mug.

She tilted her head as if waiting on him to say something.

His heart lodged in his throat. Words to continue what she started refused to come. He swallowed hard. "You were the one who wanted to talk." Okay, now he sounded like a jerk, but the hurt and guilt burned his gut.

"Oh, for the love of everything." She threw her hands up. "You're mad at me but never gave me the opportunity to tell you what happened in my own words."

"I read the report." His tone was harsher than he'd intended, but he spoke the truth.

She scowled at him. "First of all, the report states that I hadn't given the order to breach. And no, the report doesn't have details of the moments before the door blew." Anger poured off her, and she jerked her sleeve up, revealing her scars. "But trust me, I am well aware of the results."

He flinched at the force of her words.

Sally stepped to the table, glancing from him to Cassidy and back. "Sorry to interrupt." She placed their meals in front of them. "Let me know if you need anything else." She hurried away to get out of the line of fire.

"Let's get one thing straight." Cassidy stabbed her green

beans like they deserved to die. "I did not, nor would I ever, intentionally put my team in danger."

"Then what happened?" He had forgotten about the people around them and honestly didn't care.

"Amber was on one side of the door with the battering ram, McCarthy behind her, and I was on the other. I hadn't started the countdown. I was waiting for the team to get into place when Amber moved, and the world exploded." She lifted her glass. Her hands shook as she took a sip, then she wiped her mouth with her napkin. "Those moments right before the explosion..." Cassidy's eyes glazed over.

The report stated that she hadn't remembered the final moments due to trauma. "Have you tried the department psychologist to help you regain them?"

"No!" She exhaled. "No. The pain from the burns is not something I care to relive."

Kyle pondered her words. He hadn't thought of it that way. Remembering wouldn't just fill in the blanks of why Amber breached without orders. But she'd endure every moment of the pain that went with the incident. Was he that big of a jerk not to realize the physical torture she'd had to live with? "Now it's my turn to apologize."

Her brows rose to her hairline.

"Don't look at me like that." He took a bite of his hamburger and chewed, giving himself time to think before he spoke. "It hurt hearing that Amber had died. And since you were in command, my anger landed on you." *Because I didn't want to admit my own guilt.* "I never really considered anything beyond that." He should ask her about Amber's mental state that morning. But fear kept him from bringing it up. Fear that his guilt had merit.

"If you had come to see me in the hospital, you would have known."

"True. Plus, it was a childish move to change my phone

number. And that's on me. I can't say that I'm completely over the anger. I still have questions that no one can answer—except you—if you ever remember."

Cassidy looked away, refusing to make eye contact with him.

Silence stretched between them. "I'll Be Home for Christmas" played in the background, mixing with the voices of the patrons who sat, enjoying their lunches. His heart shattered at the words of the song. Amber would never again come home except in his dreams. He shook off the downward spiral.

After a moment, Cassidy met his gaze, leaned in and rested her hand on his. Her fingers were icy cold to the touch. "It's best this way. Besides, if I go there, I might never emotionally come back in one piece."

How could he argue with that? "Promise me that when the time comes, you'll try to give me the answers I'm looking for."

She started to speak, but he held up his hand.

"Not now. Someday, if you can." And someday, he'd ask her the question he was dying to know the answer to. If his words before work that morning had gotten Amber killed.

Palpable relief washed over her. "I can agree to that."

"Good. Now, let's finish and get on with our interviews." She'd surprised him with her willingness to try. Maybe it was time to come clean about his and Amber's fight that morning.

"Sounds like a plan." Cassidy smiled—really smiled—for the first time since he'd seen her again.

He liked seeing her happy. And he'd forgotten what a beautiful smile she had.

Kyle picked up a french fry and paused halfway to his mouth.

Whoa! Where had that thought come from?

SIX

The conversation with Kyle had gone better than Cassidy expected. But if he thought she'd force herself to remember the worst day of her life, he had another thing coming. Living through it once was more than enough.

She shifted in the passenger seat of his truck, finding a comfortable position as he drove to their next appointment with the witness to her cousin Laura's accident. They'd planned to leave the outlier deaths out of the equation for now, but Kyle understood her desire for answers, so he'd agreed to add Laura's case to their agenda.

"Thanks for lunch. The café has amazing food." She glanced at him and caught a slight grin that caused his dimples to appear, making him a little too appealing for her own good. A small dagger of guilt stabbed her heart. She shouldn't have those thoughts about her best friend's fiancé. Even if Amber was no longer alive.

"I'm glad you liked it. The guys and I think it's the best food around."

"You're not wrong." Her body relaxed at the easy conversation.

His gaze drifted to the rearview mirror and back to the road. "Where to?"

She flipped through the file on her lap. "There's a man in dirty clothes who looked homeless that the officer noted saw someone at the scene of Laura's accident. However, he was drunk at the time, so his statement isn't trustworthy."

"It's worth a shot." Kyle drummed his fingers on the steering wheel. "I have to admit, I haven't seen anything conclusive so far. The eyewitness to the car hijacking, the hit-and-run, along with the mother, who is adamant about her son not going on the boat without a lifejacket, gives me pause. But I'm not as convinced as you are that a serial killer connects them. I don't see it."

Yeah, she understood his dilemma. At times, she questioned herself, but her gut reaction wouldn't leave her alone.

"Let's keep at it until you have the proof you need." Cassidy refused to allow a killer to go free because of doubt, but the lack of trust in her abilities hurt. She knew it shouldn't, but it did.

He glanced at her. "I'll keep an open mind."

Those words—more than she expected—meant more than he knew. "Thanks."

His gaze drifted to the driver's side mirror, then jerked to the rearview mirror.

"Kyle?" Cassidy twisted in her seat. A large black blob floated in the air. She sucked in a breath. A drone about thirty yards back followed them. "How long has that thing been there?"

"Not long, I'm sure of that."

"Plans?"

He tossed her his cell phone. "Take a picture and send it to Doug."

Extending her arm as far as possible into the back seat to get the best shot through the rear window, she snapped several photos. Task accomplished, she sent a quick text to Doug with the images of the drone.

The wait for Kyle's partner to respond felt like an hour. The phone buzzed.

Cassidy answered the call. "Go ahead, Doug. You're on speaker."

"Get out of there. That thing is weaponized."

Kyle muttered under his breath and punched the accelerator.

The tires squealed, caught traction, and the force shoved her against the seat. "Where do you plan to go?"

"Unsure. I'm just trying to get some distance until I can find cover."

"I'm tracking your location. I'll be there soon. Stay on the line," Doug demanded.

Of course, their current path had nothing to shield them. Trees on both sides of the road, but no turn-off. Movement caught her attention. "Kyle!"

"I'm trying, Cass."

"No. The drone. It disappeared."

"What?" He scanned the rearview mirror, then ducked his head and peered out the front windshield. "Where did it go?"

They had to find it before it fired at them. Who knew what kind of weapon it possessed? "Not a clue."

"Me either." Kyle maintained his speed, and his grip on the steering wheel tightened.

"I suggest you two find it and fast."

Cassidy jumped. Her hand flew to her chest. She'd forgotten Doug was still connected.

A black shadow zoomed overhead. "There." She pointed above them.

The drone accelerated past and flipped around to face their vehicle.

"I don't like this." Kyle slowed the truck.

"What's it doing?" Doug asked.

"Hovering about fifty yards ahead."

"Not anymore." Cassidy grabbed the dashboard. "It's coming straight at us."

Kyle jammed the truck into reverse and hit the accelerator.

"Get out of the truck!" Doug's command registered, and she gripped the door handle, ready to fling it open.

"On my mark, Cass." Kyle stared at the approaching drone, one hand on the wheel, the other ready to pop the door open. He let up on the gas pedal. "Now!"

She shoved open the door and jumped. Her shoulder hit the pavement and forced her into a roll away from the vehicle. Gravel pierced her skin, and the asphalt ripped a layer from spots on her shoulder, arms and legs. Her Glock bit into her back with each rotation. She hit a bush, stopping her forward motion. Rising on her elbows, she strained to find the drone.

It dipped and slammed into the front of the truck, exploding on impact. Flames shot into the air.

Cassidy threw her arms over her head and tucked her face to the ground.

Hot air rushed over her, and debris rained down. Fragments peppered her back and legs. The heat from the fire warmed the scars on her arms, making her whimper. They didn't hurt—exactly. But the memories held pain of their own.

Her muffled hearing made distinguishing between sounds next to impossible.

"Cassidy!"

She froze and turned her ear to the sky. Nothing. Maybe she hadn't heard a voice calling out.

"Cassidy!"

Kyle. Tears pricked her eyes. The explosion hadn't killed him.

"Here." She coughed, clearing the dust and smoke from her lungs. Her ears rang with a high-pitched whistle. She lifted her head and searched for him.

He emerged from the other side of the wreckage.

She shifted and waved her hand. "Over here!"

Kyle scrambled on all fours to her. "Are you okay?"

"I think so." She pushed herself to a seated position and brushed the gravel and tiny fragments of rubble from her palms. "You?"

Confirmation that he wasn't injured never came. She lifted her gaze and gasped.

Multiple rips covered his shirt and jeans. A red mark marred his right cheek, and blood trickled down his temple. His eyes glossed over.

"Kyle." She shot out her hands to grab him before he collapsed on the pavement. "Lie down."

"I—I…um… I'm okay."

"Right." Cassidy refrained from grumbling at him and lowered him to the ground. "For once in your life, listen to reason."

His lack of protest worried her, but she was happy he hadn't fought her.

Kyle needed medical attention fast.

What happened to the phone?

She'd had it in her hand when she'd bailed from the vehicle. She scanned the area on her side of the smoking truck. There. Facedown on the gravel at the edge of the road. Cassidy stumbled over and picked it up. The screen had cracked but appeared functional.

Tires squealed, and a car door slammed.

She reached for the weapon holstered at the small of her back, her reflexes a bit slower than usual.

"Cassidy! Kyle!" Doug's voice rose over the ringing in her ears.

"Kyle needs help." She scrambled to his side.

Doug skidded to a stop. His eyes widened, then he pulled out his phone and requested an ambulance along with a firetruck. He knelt next to Kyle. "Hey there, buddy."

His gaze drifted, examining Kyle from head to toe. "Talk to me, man."

Kyle's Adam's apple bobbed. "Blown into a tree. Hit my head and back."

"Got it." Doug lifted his hand. "How many fingers am I holding up?"

"That would mean I have to open my eyes, and I'm not ready to do that yet." A lopsided smile appeared on Kyle's lips, then disappeared.

Doug chuckled. "Do it before Brent and Ethan get here, or you'll be in the hospital overnight."

Kyle groaned. "You drive a hard bargain." His eyes fluttered open, and he blinked. "Can you turn down the sun a bit?" He grimaced.

The interaction between Kyle and his partner was fascinating to watch. She wouldn't exactly call it banter, but it had a teasing tone to it.

She brushed a black wave of hair from Kyle's forehead and jerked back. The touch, a little too personal, made her want the closeness they once had shared as friends. And maybe more. "How's the headache?"

He struggled to sit up. She and Doug helped him to an upright position.

"Are you sure getting up is a smart idea?" Cassidy had no desire to see him hurt himself further.

"I'm good. Just got my bell rung, that's all." Kyle inhaled and held out a hand. Doug clasped it and pulled Kyle to his feet. Kyle used Doug's shoulder for stability until he regained his balance. "Thanks, man."

Doug patted his back. "Don't mention it."

An ambulance and several sheriff's department SUVs came to an abrupt stop.

"I'll head Brent and Ethan off at the pass as long as you promise to have them check you out and take care of that cut."

"Promise."

Doug walked away, and Kyle muttered under his breath. "Just keep that gurney away from me."

"You have something against the paramedics?"

"No. They're friends. I just hate the attention."

She'd forgotten that about him. The man disliked, with a passion, being the center of attention. Amber had once thrown him a birthday party. The results had almost turned ugly. Her friend agreed never to do it again.

Cassidy glanced up to see Dennis striding toward them. "Well, don't look now, but Sheriff Monroe is storming in this direction."

Kyle chuckled and groaned. "I've never heard anyone describe him that way."

Cassidy hoped Dennis didn't give up on her due to the safety of his officers, but she wouldn't blame him. She hated that Kyle had gotten hurt because of her.

One more thing to add to her pile of guilt.

Kyle had to admit Cassidy had provided an accurate description of his boss. Dennis *was* storming toward them.

This could get interesting.

Dennis planted himself in front of them, arms folded across his chest. "I think we can safely say that Cassidy is on to something. Serial killer? Maybe, maybe not, but someone wants her out of the picture and is willing to blow up one of my detectives doing so."

Doug rejoined them and stood off to the side. He looked like a soldier on high alert, scanning the area as if trying to detect an attack from insurgents.

Jason rushed over with Keith only steps behind. His gaze shifted from the smoldering truck to Kyle, and he raised an eyebrow. "Dude, who'd you make mad?"

"Not funny." But his lip tugged upward at his friend's

ridiculousness. "They probably thought it was you in the vehicle."

Jason placed a hand over his heart and pulled an invisible dagger from his chest. "You wound me."

"If you two are finished." Dennis looked at both of them like a father ready to reprimand a couple of young boys. He pointed at Kyle. "I want you and Cassidy checked out. Then, we're meeting at Doug's." The sheriff hitched his thumb toward Jason and Keith. "These two yahoos will get your statements, and we'll get the updates on the interviews. After that, we'll decide what happens next. I want answers." His voice softened. "I don't like my friends in danger."

"Copy that, boss." Keith nodded. "I'll go get Brent and Ethan."

Kyle watched his friend stride toward the ambulance. Might as well get it over with. "Jason, tell them we'll come to them. I don't like Cassidy being out in the open. The ambulance isn't much better, but at least she's not an easy target in there."

"Got it." Jason jogged to Keith, slapped him on the back and leaned in to relay the information, Kyle assumed.

Doug cleared his throat. "You ready to move?"

"Not really." But what choice did he have? He motioned for Cassidy to go ahead of him. "After you." His words were gruffer than intended, but his head pounded. All he wanted was a couple ibuprofens and some quiet.

Her scrutiny made him feel like an ant under a microscope. He wasn't sure if she was studying him or trying to catch him on fire.

She pivoted, held her head high and strode to the waiting paramedics.

Great. Just when they'd started to get along. His shoulders slumped. He shoved his hands in his pockets and followed.

Kyle slowed at the wreckage. The drone had flown under the engine of the truck and exploded. If they hadn't jumped from the vehicle, they would've been seriously injured or dead.

Thank You, God, for saving our lives.

His words would mean more when the gravity of the situation sank in. For now, a simple thank-you seemed in order.

He blinked away the image of the burned-out truck and continued his trek to the ambulance.

"Well, well, looks like we have another ACSD detective that decided it would be smart to go head-to-head with an explosive." Brent chuckled. "Good thing the fire department's around to patch you guys up."

Kyle rolled his eyes. "Cassidy, do you remember these two? The comedian is Brent, and his sidekick is Ethan."

"I remember." She nodded at the paramedics.

"Pleasure to see you again, ma'am." Ethan flashed a big smile and tipped an imaginary hat.

"Careful, Ethan. Don't forget, she's a Brentwood PD detective and can flatten you in one swift move," Kyle said.

Ethan waved him off. "Ignore him. Let's have a look and get the arguing about you going to the hospital over with so we can get on with our day."

Brent snickered and helped Cassidy into the back of the ambulance and out of the sight of evil eyes.

Kyle's gaze followed her. His heartbeat thumped at a rapid pace. When had she wiggled her way under his skin? His attempt to stay mad at her waned.

Ethan placed his hand on Kyle's shoulder. "She's going to be fine."

"Yeah, I know."

"You, on the other hand." Ethan glared at him.

"Do I look that bad?"

"Pretty much." The paramedic motioned him to sit on the bumper of the ambulance. Ethan removed a lollipop from his shirt pocket. "Here."

"Are you taking notes from Rachel now?" Rachel, Ethan's counterpart on the other team, kept a bag of lollipops for her younger patients.

"Quit arguing and suck on that thing. It'll help raise your blood sugar levels, plus it'll curb the nausea. You look a little green and ready to drop."

The man had a point. "Fine." Within a couple of minutes, he gained a bit of energy, and his revolting stomach had eased.

Ethan examined Kyle's back, then cleaned his wounds and butterflied the cut on his temple closed. "You're going to feel it tomorrow. I'd advise you take it easy. The hit to your head is nothing to mess around with. If your nausea doesn't go away, you see double, or any other symptoms of a concussion surface, get to the hospital."

"Yes, sir." Kyle gave the man a mock salute.

"I should have thrown you in the ambulance," Ethan grumbled while he packed up his supplies.

"I think I'll check on Cassidy." Kyle grabbed the edge of the door to boost himself inside and froze. The hair on the back of his neck stood straight. He scanned the area. Nothing appeared out of place, but his gut screamed that someone was hiding out of sight, watching, waiting, planning his next attack. And the guy had Cassidy in his crosshairs.

The priority of protecting her rose to new levels. He refused to lose someone else he cared for.

In that moment of clarity, Cassidy's life mattered to him more than he wanted to admit.

SEVEN

After a shower and a change into clean comfy clothes, Cassidy collapsed onto the sofa. The scrapes and bruises stung, but she'd gladly accept the aches when she considered the other possible outcomes.

Doug had driven her and Kyle back to his house since Kyle's truck was toast. The quiet ride seemed odd, but the reality of what happened had set in. Her own thoughts replayed the scene and how close they'd come to death. For someone who prided herself on order and perfection, how had her life spun so far out of control?

Jason's pregnant wife, Melanie, the local county coroner, strolled into the living room and held out an ice pack. "Thought you might want this."

"Thank you." Cassidy took the bag from her and sank deeper into the couch. Now that the adrenaline had faded, the bruises she'd acquired tumbling from the vehicle seemed to have multiplied.

"Here, I figured you could use some caffeine too." Melanie handed her a can of Pepsi.

She accepted and took a sip. The bubbles coated her throat and soothed her battered nerves. "This is perfect."

Melanie smiled. "You looked like you needed a little sugary comfort."

"What about you?" Cassidy pointed to the yellowish

liquid in Melanie's glass. "That does not look like caffeinated goodness."

"The one bad thing about pregnancy. No caffeine. Besides, I'm sticking with ginger ale. My stomach's been a little queasy today." Melanie braced one hand on the arm of the other end of the couch and lowered herself onto the cushion. "The guys will join us soon. They're in the kitchen arguing over who's going to win the next football game or some such nonsense. I think they're bleeding off the stress from the attack and what could've happened without saying so."

"I haven't known them long, but I'd say that sounds right."

"My guess is that it won't take long before they'll plan what to do next to protect you." Melanie took a sip.

"I can't believe they're willing to help me. I'm sure Kyle hasn't had nice things to say these past few months." The fact the team hadn't glared at her and told her to leave continued to surprise her.

Melanie set her glass on the end table and shifted to face her. "He hasn't said much at all. Granted, I'm new to the scene, but I was here when his fiancée died. She was your partner, right?"

Cassidy fiddled with the bag of ice on her old burn scars. The heat from the garage apartment fire and the truck explosion had left her old injury an angry red. "Yes."

"And I'm guessing that happened at the same time?" Melanie pointed to her arm.

"Yes." Her answer barely above a whisper.

"Want to talk about it?"

Not really. But Cassidy supposed it might do her good to confide in someone. Her mother and father had passed away years ago, and now her best friend and her cousin were both gone. She had no one left to talk to about all the personal stuff. She got along great with her coworkers, but it wasn't the same as a family or a best friend.

She picked at the hem of her oversize T-shirt. "I led the raid that killed Amber."

"And let me guess, Kyle blames you."

Cassidy's jaw dropped. She jerked her gaze to Melanie. How did she know that?

"Oh, please. If I've learned anything about these guys, it's that they feel deeply. They won't admit it, and ergo, they have to blame someone for the hurt." Melanie retrieved her glass, lifted it and shrugged. "And sometimes it's to hide their own guilt."

"Maybe it was my fault. The last few seconds before the explosion… Everyone says the same thing. Amber breached early." Cassidy scraped her teeth across her lower lip. "I've read the report, but those last moments are a blank. If I could remember…"

"But you don't want to relive it."

Unable to speak, Cassidy shook her head.

"Look. You probably don't know this, but I've been where you are. Not being able to remember—not wanting to remember. The idea of opening that wound is terrifying."

Cassidy couldn't disagree with that last statement.

"But sometimes it's healing." Voices drifted in from the kitchen, and Melanie glanced over her shoulder, then back to Cassidy. "If you ever need a listening ear, I'm here for you."

Cassidy blinked back the tears threatening to fall. Maybe she should ask Melanie for advice. She hadn't had a confidante in six months. The gesture gave her hope that life might return to normal—someday. "Thank you. I really appreciate that."

Melanie smiled. "I have a feeling that you and I have a lot in common."

Before she could respond, the guys came in and joined them.

"Sit down. You're hobbling worse than Judith's boyfriend, Harold, after his knee replacement surgery." Jason pointed Kyle toward the recliner and gave him a gentle push.

Kyle grimaced as he sat and leaned back. "Stupid tree." He stuffed the throw pillow behind the small of his back.

Keith and Doug chuckled and found extra chairs to pull into a circle with the couch and recliner.

"You better hope that ibuprofen kicks in before Dennis sees you, or you'll end up with a hospital stay." Keith grinned.

The front door clicked shut. "Did I hear my name?" Sheriff Dennis Monroe waltzed in, laptop tucked under his arm.

"Nope. Not at all." Kyle's upbeat tone amused her.

"Liar." Doug coughed out the word, and Kyle scowled at him.

Dennis clapped a hand on Kyle's shoulder. "Are you sure about that?"

Kyle cringed and groaned.

"That's what I thought." Dennis shook his head and muttered, "Why is it my detectives act like children?"

"You know you love them." Melanie grinned and rubbed her pregnant belly.

"Don't remind me." The sheriff took an open seat. "I'll deal with Kyle later. Mel, how are you feeling? Charlotte wants an update."

Melanie smiled. "Ready for Baby Cooper to make his or her appearance."

"When do you go on maternity leave?"

"Three more days. Good thing too. I can't reach over the little one anymore."

Dennis chuckled. "I'll tell Charlotte to expect a call for breakfast soon."

"Yes, please."

"Perfect. Now, let's talk about the interviews." Dennis propped his ankle across his knee.

Cassidy found it fascinating that the sheriff took care of his deputies and asked about their significant others before focusing on work. The man truly was an amazing boss. She wondered what it would be like to work for him.

Relieved to put emotions aside, she jumped at the offer to discuss the case. "We talked with Ms. Perkins about her son Aaron's drowning. She's still adamant about him always wearing a life jacket. I believe her. But you already know that." She refrained from adding anything about a serial killer.

"Kyle, what do you think?" Dennis asked.

"The woman was convincing. I'm leaning toward it not being an accident. But he had a trauma as a child and saw a therapist, so we need to consider that. We have a lead on a friend that went boating with him the day before, but his office admin said he was traveling today. Law enforcement never interviewed the friend. With it seeming like an accident, we don't think they did much digging. I'd like to see what the friend says about Aaron's habits and mental state. Plus, if we could find his body, it might clarify our questions."

Keith halted his coffee cup halfway to his mouth. "Mental state? Are you thinking suicide?"

"Not really, but I'd like to rule it out," Kyle said.

The sheriff scratched his jaw. "I'll put in a request for the divers to do another search once spring arrives. Until then, I'd like a little more information from people who knew Aaron to corroborate Mrs. Perkins's claims. Keep digging into that case. What else do you have?"

Kyle shifted, his movements stilted. "Mr. Morrison had nothing major to add to his witness statement on the shooting. He did mention the impression of the shooter being a homeless man. As for his hit-and-run, nothing new there. However, we had a twist that I hadn't seen coming. Aaron's friend Robert Hansen works for Morrison."

"When did that happen?" Jason squeezed Melanie's hand.

"About a year ago," Kyle said.

"Interesting timing." Keith tipped back and rocked on the two legs of the chair.

"Makes sense, though. Hansen went to college with Aaron. They both majored in computer engineering."

Cassidy scrunched her forehead. The picture on the mantel bothered her, but the why eluded her.

"Want to let us in on what has you scowling?" Melanie asked.

She blinked and scanned the group. They all stared at her. "What? Did I miss something?"

Dennis rested his elbows on his knees. A position she'd come to recognize as his serious pose. "I asked if you had another impression about Mr. Morrison."

"Sorry. I zoned out there for a second."

"Want to share with the class?" Jason grinned.

"Mrs. Morrison had a picture of her husband and his business partners from when they started their company that caught my eye. They were young. I almost didn't recognize John Morrison." Her teeth scraped her lower lip. "I know from searching the website that he's the sole owner now. The other partners looked familiar, but why?"

The taps of a keyboard filled the otherwise quiet room. Doug looked up from the laptop. "That's because you know them. Well, you know *of* them." He tapped the screen. "Try Aaron Perkins and Sandy and Michael Hughes."

Kyle jolted. "Our drowning victim and the couple shot in the carjacking?"

"The same," Doug said.

Cassidy's jaw dropped. "I've done a web search on the start of the tech company and never found any reference of their names. It just stated friends."

"Someone didn't want the names connected. Whoever it was had mad computer skills and buried the original information about the company. It's there, but it took some serious digging."

"Mr. Morrison never said a word about the three of them." Cassidy tucked a flyaway strand of hair behind her ear. "We found out Aaron worked there, but not that he was a partner."

"Makes you wonder why he didn't mention it." Dennis exhaled. "I think we'd better do a deep dive into Mr. Morrison."

Doug waved a hand like swatting a fly. "I'll take that assignment."

"It's yours." Dennis jotted a note on his pad of paper. "Next."

"I'd like to know what Jason found out about our homeless guy who Morrison saw at the scene of the shooting." Keith took a swig of the Pepsi he'd brought from the kitchen and set it on the floor next to his chair.

"He had no recollection of the crime. The officer said he was high at the time, so it's not surprising he has no memory of it," Jason said.

Cassidy grabbed a notepad from the coffee table and scribbled down questions and thoughts. "How was he when you talked to him? High or sober?"

"Sober. He says he's clean and has been for three months."

"Do you believe him?" Dennis asked.

"His Narcotics Anonymous sponsor stayed with him

during the interview. The man vouched for him. I have no reason to doubt he told me the truth." Jason shrugged.

Cassidy's mind whirled. "Could he have shot Sandy and Michael?"

"It's possible, I guess. The officers recovered the weapon. The killer threw it into the car after shooting Mr. and Mrs. Hughes." Jason shifted to face Melanie. "And before you ask. No prints were found."

Melanie scrunched her nose at her husband. "Fine."

"I reinterviewed two out of the three families on my list. The other family was out of town." Keith referred to his notes. "I also revisited the officer who wrote the report on the strangulation victim you assigned me. She told me that the scene had a *weird vibe*. Her words, not mine. But the sparse evidence left them without a suspect. She also worked the drive-by shooting in the same area. The official statement says possibly gang related. She disagreed but had no proof to refute the report."

"Does the officer think it's the same killer?" Doug asked.

"She didn't go as far as to say that. But when I asked, she shrugged and said it had crossed her mind. No evidence, but a strong gut feeling from a seasoned officer..." Keith let the words hang in the air.

He continued to fill everyone in on the interview he'd conducted with the second victim's family.

Cassidy's mind wandered. She hadn't heard about the officer's concerns, which added to her theory. Did Keith's area and her and Kyle's area link together like she'd thought? But the association between Morrison, Perkins and the Hugheses grabbed her attention. Would Mr. Morrison lie about the shooting and the hit-and-run? Not unless he was the killer. Was it possible? She heard Doug's voice, but his words didn't register. If the homeless man shot the couple, the link between the cases and her serial killer idea disintegrated. She guessed it was conceivable Morrison had other reasons for not admitting his connection to the others.

"I'm starting to agree with Cassidy."

"What?" She jerked her attention to Doug. Had she heard him correctly?

"I said I think you're on to something with the cases being connected." Doug tilted his head. "Why are you surprised?"

Her shoulders slumped. "No one has agreed with me so far, and my department thinks I've lost it. I guess I expected you all to brush off my theory."

Doug placed his laptop on the coffee table. "I hadn't planned to, but I looked into one of the other victims that didn't fit into the cluster, similar to Cassidy's cousin. The file says the woman committed suicide, but after talking with her family and friends, I'm not sure I agree with the findings. Nothing in her life points to that, but that doesn't mean it didn't happen that way. Families tend to defend their loved ones. I just have a lot of questions."

Cassidy's spine melted into the couch. They hadn't dismissed her belief. "I can't thank you enough for continuing to investigate. I really do think this is something bigger than it appears."

"I'm not fully bought off on one person being responsible for all these deaths, but I believe the ones we've reopened aren't what they seem." Doug rubbed the back of his neck. "And the possibility of a connection… I'm not ruling it out."

"I'd say we have reason to keep investigating." Dennis's gaze landed on her. "I'm sorry we can't fully agree with your serial killer theory."

She wanted to hug the man for not ignoring her opinion. "As long as you're willing to keep investigating, I'm grateful." She glanced at Kyle, desperate to ask his opinion. But the man appeared ready to drop, so she'd keep the question to herself until later.

Keith crossed his arms over his chest. "Let's pull Amy in and have her analyze the photos from each crime, and see what her photographer's eye finds."

"I'm going to have to put your wife on the payroll if we keep pulling her in on our cases," Dennis grumbled. But Cassidy figured the sheriff only protested for the sake of protesting.

Keith smiled. "As much as I'd love her working with us, she kind of has her hands full with Connor and her own business."

Melanie chuckled. "No doubt. The woman barely has time to breathe."

"I'm hoping she'll slow down a bit and take it easy in the near future." Keith's gaze dropped to Melanie's belly and back up.

Had anyone else noticed where his eyes had gone? Did he and Amy have news, or was he thinking about the future?

Cassidy cleared her throat, and the group turned to her. "I'm sorry to interrupt, but Melanie, I have a question about my cousin's case."

"Go for it."

"The preliminary statement indicated Laura's blood alcohol level. Did you look at the full report?"

Melanie struggled to grab her messenger bag off the floor.

"I've got it, babe." Jason retrieved the bag and handed it to his wife.

"Thanks. Your son or daughter is making it hard for me to move."

Jason splayed his hand over her nine-month-pregnant belly. "I guess I'll have to talk with him or her about that."

A weight landed on Cassidy's chest. She wanted what Melanie had. A husband. A helper in life. Someone to cherish her. Her father had loved her in his own way, but treasured her? No. The man had pushed her to excellence and had demanded perfection.

She swallowed and willed back the tears threatening to fall. A scan of the room spoke volumes. Dennis and Keith smiled. Kyle closed his eyes and gave a slight shake of his head. But it was Doug who broke her heart. He looked away, refusing to watch the interaction. So many emotions. All for different reasons.

"Give me a second to read through the file." Melanie flipped through the document. The rest of the room stayed quiet, waiting for her to finish. "Huh."

"What is it?" Kyle asked.

"The labs came back, but due to the officers closing the case, I doubt anyone rushed to look at them."

"And?" Jason prodded.

"Laura's BAL was high. Very high. But her stomach contents indicated no alcohol."

Dennis stood and moved behind Melanie. "How is that possible?" He leaned over her shoulder to read the file.

Melanie pointed at the paper. "See?"

"May I?" Dennis held out his hand.

"Of course." Melanie gave the sheriff the file.

Dennis studied the report for several minutes. "I want Laura's case officially reopened. Kyle, you and Cassidy go to the impound lot and take another look at the car. I want new pictures of the interior and exterior. Go through that thing from top to bottom."

"Anything specific we're looking for?" Kyle asked.

The sheriff shook his head. "No. But I'll give up my vacation time if you don't find evidence that VSPD missed in the original investigation. I'll take care of jurisdiction issues. I doubt the chief of police will have a problem handing us the case."

"Will do." Kyle grinned. "I'd hate for you to lose your time off."

Dennis chuckled. "Charlotte might make me sleep in the doghouse if I do."

"We can't have that." Kyle turned serious, and his gaze met Cassidy's. "Don't worry. We'll do it right."

Her heart warmed at his determination on her behalf.

Was it too much to ask for him to treat her like the friends they used to be?

The bruise on Kyle's back ached, and the cut on his head stung. But only by the grace of God had he and Cassidy survived the drone attack.

After agreeing to continue their investigations tomorrow, Jason took Melanie home to rest, and Dennis followed behind to join his wife and daughters for dinner.

Kyle walked Keith to the door and stood, hand on its edge, as he lowered his voice. "Did you finish your assessment?"

"I did." Keith grabbed his coat from the hook.

"And?"

"I found nothing that leads me to think someone from an old case or an ex-boyfriend is out to get Cassidy."

"No one?"

"Nope. I'm still digging, but I think I'm going in the wrong direction."

"That leaves random, or did she stumble upon something?"

"My skepticism says there's no serial killer, but she is

right about one thing…there are too many holes. There's something about each case that feels wrong."

Kyle hadn't expected to agree, but he'd be stupid not to at least entertain the idea.

Keith zipped his coat and stepped outside. "Call if you need anything."

"You know I will."

His friend turned to face him. "I know a bit of what you're going through, and it's not easy to ask for help or admit your own struggles. Please don't make the same mistakes I did."

The muscles in Kyle's neck eased. His friend cared. And he appreciated it. "Thanks. I promise I'll ask for help if I need it."

Keith gave a quick nod. "Good enough. See you tomorrow."

"Tell Amy and Connor hi for me."

A smile graced his friend's face. "Absolutely." Keith jogged to his SUV and waved as he pulled from the driveway.

Kyle shut the door, flipped the lock and set the alarm. Not for the first time, he was grateful for the high-level security system Doug had installed.

Since the group discussion, his worry had skyrocketed. Had a serial killer fooled all those law enforcement officers? Would his team be able to stop him? Or was someone else targeting her, and would they find him or her in time to keep Cassidy alive? He'd leave that concern for tomorrow. Tonight, he needed time to recuperate.

He ambled to his seat and collapsed in the chair. His muscles had stiffened, making it difficult to move without thought.

God, I don't think I've thanked You enough for protect-

*ing us today. So, thank You again. But if You could make
the bruises ache less, I'd appreciate it.*

Pots and pans clanked, and "Silent Night" on the radio
filtered in from the kitchen. Doug had disappeared in there
a while ago, leaving Kyle to finish saying goodbye to their
friends. He should go help, but his energy level had hit
zero. He wanted to blame his injuries, but worry about
Cassidy had sneaked in and taken hold.

"Doug said he'd make dinner while we rest."

Kyle glanced up and found Cassidy watching him. "He's
a good guy."

"That he is. A bit quiet and a little serious, but I can tell
he's a good friend."

"A great friend and partner." Kyle sighed. "He's an in-
trovert by nature, but circumstances have played a role in
that as well."

"After what you told me, I'm not surprised." Cassidy
scooted farther into the couch and held a throw pillow in
her lap. "Is that why you're more serious now? Circumstances?"

He opened his mouth then closed it. It was more than
that. Now that he sat alone in the living room with Cassidy, uncertainty about what to say had dug in its claws.
Dennis had encouraged him to clear the air between them,
but doing so meant fessing up to his role on that horrible
day. Did he dare go there?

*God, Dennis was right. I need to put the past behind
me and be the friend Cassidy needs. If You don't mind, I
need Your strength.*

The apology teetered on his tongue but refused to fall.
Come on, man up and say it. He sighed. "Cassidy." Wow,
this was harder than he'd imagined.

She tilted her head. "Yes."

"I'm sorry. I shouldn't have blamed you for Amber's

death. Since you commanded the raid, it made it easy to place the responsibility on you. I never should have done that." The guilt gnawed at his gut. He needed to explain why. But the words soured in his throat.

Cassidy's jaw dropped, and she stared at him. "I—I'm not sure what to say. Thank you for that. It couldn't have been easy."

A humorless laugh escaped. "Not at all. But there's more."

"Kyle. We had a great friendship before Amber's death. I haven't forgotten that. I hope you haven't either."

"Maybe for a moment—a nine-month moment." He smiled.

"If I could, I'd bring Amber back to you. But I can't."

"I know. Deep down, I've always known. It's my own guilt that kept me from acknowledging that."

Cassidy picked up the hot tea Doug had brought her when the others left and cradled the mug in her hands. "Want to talk about it?"

Did he? He owed it to Cassidy to come clean. "I might have played a role in Amber's death."

She lifted her cup to her lips and froze. "And how do you think you did that?"

Kyle ran a hand through his hair. "Remember how I said hateful words to my parents before they died in a car accident?"

She took a sip of her tea and nodded.

"I did the same thing with Amber that day." He swallowed hard.

Tears swam in Cassidy's eyes. "I know."

"If I had kept my angry words to myself… Wait, you do?"

"She was my best friend. Of course she told me about your argument."

Kyle cringed. "I said things I regret."

"Making her choose between her job and having kids? What were you thinking?" Her words held no bite but a kindness he hadn't deserved.

He lowered his head and ran a hand through his hair. "I'd spent the night before consoling a Valley Springs PD officer's children. She'd made a normal traffic stop, and an oncoming car clipped her as she walked back to her cruiser." He blew out a long breath.

"Did she make it?"

"Yes. And she's recovered and is back at work. But it shook me up thinking about Amber and when we had kids." He pinched the bridge of his nose.

"I wanted to clock you for hurting my best friend, but it all makes more sense now."

He hoped she understood, but still, it was no excuse for what he'd done. "It was my fault, not yours, that Amber died."

Cassidy straightened in her seat. "Why on earth would you say that?"

"Because my angry words had to have taken her focus off of the job."

She shook her head. "Kyle. Amber knew you loved her. She told me that morning that she was worried about you. You hadn't explained, and she wondered what had happened."

"What if it took her focus off the raid? And that's why she breached early?"

Cassidy stared at her hands. "I don't know the reason why she did it, but I'm confident her concentration was on the job."

"That helps my guilt a bit. But I want to know why." Kyle hated asking Cassidy. She'd been through enough pain.

"Someday the final pieces will fall into place. The memories are buried in here somewhere." She tapped her temple. "I just can't go there—not yet. It's too real. The times I've tried—I feel the heat on my skin. Smell the fire." She shook her head and took another sip of her hot tea.

The agony she endured that day had left scars, physical and emotional. He refused to cause her more pain. "Can we try to find our way back to our friendship?"

"I'd like that—a lot. I've missed you."

Kyle's heart beat a little too fast for her simple words. "Me too."

Amber would be proud of him for letting go of his anger, but would she be happy that his feelings for Cassidy had risen above a friendship?

His gaze locked with hers. Did she feel the pull between them too?

Doug poked his head into the living room. "Dinner in five."

"Thanks. We'll be there." He forced himself to look away from Cassidy. He stood and held out his hand. "We don't want to keep Doug waiting."

She accepted his gesture and rose to her feet. "I'm glad we talked. I hope it helped."

"It did." A little too much.

He glanced at the keypad by the front door, confirming he'd engaged the security system.

The task of keeping Cassidy alive had an all-new meaning, and he refused to fail.

EIGHT

The seat belt of Kyle's rental truck cut into Cassidy's sore shoulder. Her aches and pains from yesterday had dulled, but the reality of what had happened stuck with her.

Two times in her life, she'd come close to being blown up. This time she'd walked away with minor injuries. She flexed her hand, and her scarred skin pulled tight. A memory she'd love to forget.

I owe You a thanks, God. But I have to admit, it's hard to feel You close after all that's happened. Why are You so far away?

The explosion that took Amber's life had wreaked havoc on Cassidy's faith. She'd struggled to step foot in church. And her prayers felt like yelling down a long tunnel. The closeness she'd had with God had disappeared. For the life of her, she had no idea how to regain the intimate relationship with Him that she once had.

"We'll be at the impound yard in about ten minutes." Kyle adjusted the temperature of the vehicle. "Is that better?"

She glanced at him and back to the window. "It's fine, thanks." Her dilemma with God plagued her. She'd witnessed the ACSD group's faith and had heard about their struggles. Why couldn't she find her way back?

Buildings became sparse as they drove, giving way to a mix of open land and clusters of trees.

The knot in Cassidy's stomach twisted tighter the closer they got. She hadn't anticipated the impact that seeing her cousin's wrecked car would have on her. Her time in the hospital and then work hadn't allowed her the opportunity to examine the vehicle. She'd barely made it to Laura's funeral. *Compartmentalize, girl.* That's what she did on duty when tragedy stuck, and now she had to lean on that skill if she had any hope of not falling apart.

She straightened. "What do you make of the autopsy report?"

Kyle glanced at her. "The conflicting report of her BAL and no alcohol in her stomach?"

"It seems impossible, doesn't it?"

"Can't say I've heard of it happening before, but there has to be an explanation." He drummed the steering wheel with his fingers. "Do you have any ideas?"

Cassidy shook her head. "I was hoping you did."

He chuckled. "If there's anything to find, the lab rats will find it."

"I still can't believe y'all call them that." The more she heard about the sheriff's department, the more it fascinated her. Rigid rules and seriousness no longer had the same appeal.

"They're the best. And with Melanie overseeing them, it takes it to a whole new level."

"Let's hope we have something new for them to analyze." Hope. There that word was again. The lack of hope in her life squeezed her heart. Someday it would return—maybe.

Kyle parked across the street from Ben's Body Shop. "The yard is over there." He pointed to an area to the side and behind the business.

Her jaw dropped at the single building with a small parking lot in front. Trees leading to a wooded area lined a large fenced-in section behind the shop. The place wasn't remote but had a secluded feel to it. She had a hard time believing that the county didn't have a place near the sheriff's office. "This is the department's impound yard?"

He grinned. "And VSPD's. Ben is ex-army. He services all the vehicles and takes care of the yard. It's a nice gig for him, and his security is tight, so the departments benefit too. Plus, when Doug joined the department, Ben had him come out and ramp up the system."

"Sounds like it's a win-win situation."

"It really is." Kyle tugged a tissue paper square from his pocket. "Don't get mad, but I have something for you."

"O-kay." She drew out the word.

"I'd like you to wear this." He handed her the paper, which held a small item. "It has a GPS inside."

"Kyle."

"Hear me out. Whoever is out to get you is determined. If we get separated, I want a way to find you."

The man was treading on her independence, but how could she argue? The danger was real. She unwrapped the item. A gold chain with a cross pendant stared back at her. "It's beautiful."

A lopsided grin graced his face. "It reminded me of you."

She put it on and tucked the cross inside her shirt. "Thank you for taking the precaution."

Kyle shrugged and rested his hand on the door handle. "Ready?"

"Sure." Cassidy zipped her coat and pulled on her gloves. When she opened the passenger side, the cold air whipped her hair across her face. She hooked her finger around the strand and tucked it behind her ear. "I think the temps have dropped even lower instead of warming this morning."

Bundled up and evidence kit in hand, Kyle waited for her to join him, then crossed the street. "I heard on the news last night that we might get a white Christmas."

"I'm not sure I'm ready for the holidays, but I guess I don't have a choice."

Kyle grew quiet, lost in his own thoughts. Due to his parents' car accident on Christmas Eve, Cassidy knew through their previous conversations that this time of year brought up bad memories.

She placed a gloved hand on his forearm. "You okay?"

He blinked. "Yeah, let's go."

The hope he'd open up dissolved. But he had his reasons. She longed for the day that he'd trust her again.

They crossed the street and stepped onto the sidewalk next to the body shop's tiny parking lot, which consisted of four spots. All of which were full. She assumed with vehicles waiting for service or for owners to come and pick them up.

"We need to go inside. I have to check in with Ben to gain access to the car." Kyle motioned to the entrance.

"Not a problem." Cassidy halted. "I forgot the file. It's on the passenger seat. Go on, I'll be back in a minute."

"That's okay. I'll wait." Kyle clicked the fob and unlocked the doors.

Cassidy jogged to the truck. Her muscles ached from the day before, but she pushed forward. She opened the driver's door, leaned across the console and snagged the file she'd copied that morning for reference. She crawled out and waved the documents. "Got it."

After closing the door and hearing Kyle click the locks with the car fob, she headed across the two-lane street.

An engine revved to her right.

She glanced in the direction of the sound.

A dark SUV picked up speed and aimed straight toward her.

She stood in the middle of the road, her brain frozen and her limbs numb. Her vision tunneled on the vehicle barreling toward her. She hyperfocused on the black bars of the grille guard. Her brain shouted at her to get out of the way, but her body refused to comply.

Cassidy forced her legs to move. She took two steps. The realization that she couldn't escape struck her. She screamed.

"Cassidy!"

The force of the hit threw her across the road. Her body bounced. A hard object landed on top of her.

The engine rumbled and disappeared.

She tried to breathe, but her lungs refused to expand. Black dots swarmed behind her eyelids, and the world grew dark.

God, help me. I don't want to die.

Kyle's arms and legs trembled.

He'd seen the SUV coming straight at Cassidy and sprinted toward her, tackling her at the last moment. A second longer, they both would have been the victim of a hit-and-run.

"Cassidy?" He rolled off her. "Cassidy, talk to me."

"Help is on the way." Kyle glanced up to see Ben standing over him. "Anything I can do?"

Kyle hadn't heard Ben approach, but he appreciated the man's quick thinking. "Did you get a license plate?"

"No, but my cameras pointing at the street should give us that." Ben jutted his chin at Cassidy. "You tackle like a linebacker. Your lady's gonna feel it tomorrow."

His lady? His gaze traveled to Cassidy. He brushed the

hair from her face and checked her pulse. A steady thump met his fingertips. "I hope I didn't crack a rib."

"Better than dead." Ben had a point.

"True." Kyle cupped her cheek, careful not to touch the new scrape she'd acquired. "Cassidy, honey, wake up. Tell me you're okay."

She groaned, and her eyes fluttered open. "Kyle?" she gasped.

"I'm right here." He clasped her fingers.

"Can't. Breathe."

Kyle's hand shook as he ran his gaze over her looking for a serious injury. "Ben, I need help now!"

"Easy there, buddy." Ben crouched on the other side of Cassidy. "I think she got the wind knocked out of her."

Please, God, let it be that.

"Try to breathe deep." Kyle's voice quavered, but he didn't care. She could have died.

She nodded. After a couple of minutes, her breathing evened out. "The car hit me."

He shook his head. "No, Cass. That was me. I'm sorry if I hurt you."

"'S okay." Her words slurred a bit as she continued to struggle with her breathing. She took in a lungful of air. "Thank you."

"Glad to help." He smiled.

Her brows pulled together. "You're bleeding."

He scanned his arms and torso. A blotch of red grew in diameter on his shirt. He'd taken her to the ground, and his side had taken the brunt of the force against the concrete curb. "I must have scraped it."

Ben grunted.

So maybe he had a gash, but he refused to worry Cassidy.

Multiple sirens whined, then shut off. The red-and-blue

lights of the fire engine and ambulance flashed in the parking lot and on the street. "The cavalry is coming."

She fought to sit up.

"Please, stay down."

"No. I want up."

Kyle wanted to scold her, but he knew his efforts would be worthless. "Hold on. Let us help." He and Ben helped Cassidy to a seated position.

"Thanks." The gratefulness in her eyes melted the remaining ice around his heart.

The guys helped Cassidy to sit on the curb. The new position eased the pull on her back. She brought her knees up and rested her arms on them. Dirt covered her clothes and skin, and her hair had to have a medusa vibe. She looked a mess.

But her aching ribs had her attention. And she sported more scrapes to add to her previous ones. Sleeping for a week sounded wonderful. But with a killer on the loose, she had to force her injuries to the back of her mind and continue her hunt for justice.

"Well, well, well, we meet again." Ethan sat on his haunches. "Heard you tried to go *mano y mano* with an SUV."

"So now you speak Spanish?" The man amused her with his nonchalant attitude.

"Not hardly." He grinned at her.

"Your information is wrong. I—" she pointed at herself "—tried to escape the person trying to kill me." Cassidy's gaze drifted to Kyle. "But if Kyle hadn't tackled me and pushed me out of the way…"

"I get it." Ethan softened his tone. "You don't have to say it."

She swallowed the growing lump in her throat.

The teasing timbre she'd come to associate with the paramedic returned. "How do you want to do this? Want to tell me what hurts, or what doesn't hurt?"

Cassidy rolled her eyes.

"Well?"

"I'm thinking." She smirked.

He laughed and retrieved his stethoscope from his bag. With a flick, he looped it around his neck.

"Let's go with what hurts. My ribs and new scrapes on my arms and forehead."

"I'll take a look at those ribs and clean you up. When I'm done, I'll find the paperwork."

She arched a brow. "No begging me to go to the hospital?"

Ethan shook his head. "Nope. That's a waste of breath."

"True." She held her palms up. "Go for it."

"Ribs first. If I think they're broken, I'm calling for reinforcements, and you'll get that trip in my sweet ride over there."

"I hate to break it to you, but an ambulance is not sweet."

"You wound me." He huffed. Ethan poked at her sore ribs.

She winced at the pressure, but overall, the pain only hit a four or five on her ten-point scale.

"I believe you only bruised them. They'll hurt but aren't life-threatening."

"Good." The last thing she wanted was Kyle feeling guilty about a serious injury.

"Although, I want it on record that only an X-ray will confirm my diagnosis." He arranged the saline, gauze and bandages for easy access. "Let's take a look at those hands."

She obliged, and Ethan got busy treating her other injuries.

Ignoring the sting that accompanied Ethan's actions, she searched for Kyle.

When she spotted him, her breath caught. Blood soaked his shirt, and a gash marred his side.

Kyle had saved her life. For that, she'd forever be grateful.

The open wound where Kyle had hit the concrete curb smarted like a thousand bee stings. Not to mention the ache in his ribs. But he'd suffer the severest of injuries to keep Cassidy safe.

Brent ripped open a package of gauze, soaked it in saline solution and cleaned the gash.

Kyle sucked in air between his teeth. "I'm starting to think Sheriff Monroe is right. Rachel has a better bedside manner."

"Rachel and Peter aren't on shift today, so you're stuck with us." Brent wiped around the cut.

"Oh, yay. I'm so excited."

The paramedic scowled at him. "Sarcasm is not going to get you better treatment. What's up with you anyway?"

"I have no idea what you're talking about?"

Brent dabbed at his gash. "Oh, please."

Kyle scowled. "Take it easy, man."

"Wimp."

"I was kidding before, but you really don't have any bedside manner, do you?" He peered over Brent's shoulder. The bright red scrapes on Cassidy's arm and the darkening bruise on her cheek sent a wave of guilt zipping through him.

"From what I've heard, if you hadn't tackled her, she'd be a goner."

Kyle blinked and returned his focus to Brent. "What?"

The paramedic rolled his eyes and gestured toward Cassidy. "Rumor has it you two aren't exactly friends, but from where I sit, you've got it bad."

"I—I…" The denial hung on his lips. "She used to be Amber's best friend and, by default, mine. We're finding our way back to that friendship, but nothing more will ever come of it."

Brent shook his head. "You keep telling yourself that."

He glanced at Cassidy again, and his stomach did that funny flip-flop like it used to with Amber. No. He didn't have *those kinds of feelings* for Cassidy and never would. He shifted his gaze to the spot where he'd almost lost her, then his attention drifted back to her. Right?

Brent snickered as he butterflied the cut closed. "There ya go. Good as new."

"Thanks." Kyle straightened his shirt. The blood-soaked material had turned sticky. A clean shirt—he glanced down, taking note of the rip in the side of his jeans—and new pants were in order.

The paramedic seemed to notice the direction of Kyle's thoughts. "I can't help you in the jeans department, but I have an extra Valley Springs Fire Department T-shirt in the medic unit."

"Me? Be seen in a VSFD shirt? I don't know, man. It could ruin my image."

"Ha ha. Very funny." Brent folded his arms across his chest, trying hard to hide his smirk. "Do you want it or not?"

Kyle rested a hand on Brent's shoulder. "I'd appreciate it."

A few moments and a clean shirt later, he thanked his friend, and they joined Ethan and Cassidy.

"Everything okay over here?" Kyle searched her features for the truth.

"I'm fine. Ethan here is playing mother hen."

Ethan sighed. "You two are horrible patients."

"Thank you."

"Truth." Kyle and Cassidy spoke in unison.

The paramedics chuckled and gathered their gear.

"We're here if you need anything." Ethan paused and studied them. "But I'd prefer not getting an emergency call again."

Kyle nodded. "You and me both."

With the papers signed, the men loaded the ambulance and took off.

Ben had returned inside, and the guys had left, leaving only a couple of crime scene techs to finish up. The busyness of the scene had died down to an eerie silence.

The evidence kit lay where he'd dropped it over an hour ago. The daunting task of examining Laura's car still loomed ahead.

With a quick glance at the bloodstain—his bloodstain—on the pavement, the realization of how close they'd come to serious injury or death kicked in. His pulse rate quickened.

He'd risked his life for the woman he'd loathed for the past year. But he had to be honest with himself. He'd do it again if it meant protecting Cassidy.

NINE

Cassidy dusted off the remaining dirt from her close call and followed Kyle into the body shop. The smell of solvent mixed with paint turned her stomach, sending her back in time to her father's garage. He loved to tinker with cars when he returned from deployment. But he never let her touch his prized possessions after she'd made a mistake.

She'd sloshed oil onto his current car project, and he banned her from assisting him ever again. It didn't matter that the oil spots wiped off. It was the principle of the thing. Her lack of perfection had disappointed him. His high expectations and demand for excellence had put a wedge between them. But even to this day, she measured her success by his standards. That was one of the reasons why losing Amber had sent her reeling. Her team had gotten hurt. She'd failed as the commander of the raid.

"Cassidy?"

She glanced up and found Kyle staring at her.

"Are you okay? Ben asked you a question."

Cassidy shook off the path of her thoughts and shifted her gaze to Ben. "I'm sorry. What did you say?"

"I asked how you are feeling, but I think you answered my question."

She waved him off. "My body is complaining, and I'll really feel it tomorrow, but I'm good."

"Then what had you so deep in thought?" Kyle asked.

"This—" she motioned to the shop "—reminds me of my father."

"Obviously, not in a good way." Ben opened a lock box and handed Kyle a key. "Why don't you sign the impound log and get her away from those memories."

Heat crept up her neck. "Thanks, Ben."

Kyle studied her, then signed for the key. "We'll be back in a bit."

"Take your time. I'll be here all afternoon." With that, Ben ambled through the doorway to the main work area.

"Are you ready for this?" Kyle's concern sent emotions flooding her system.

Cassidy stood tall. "If I want to find her killer, I have to be."

"Then let's get to it." After protesting her comment about a killer, he opened the door and motioned for her to go first.

She brushed past him and stepped outside. The bright sun chased away the darkness that had taken up residence.

Kyle checked the tag on the key. "Says slot 12B." He pointed to the section of vehicles to the left.

The woods butted up against the fence that separated the lot from the outside world. A roll of barbed wire rested on top of the chain-link barrier, keeping an intruder from climbing over. But it didn't shield from prying eyes. Her steps faltered. "Do you think he's still out there?"

Kyle stopped next to her. "Your attacker?"

She nodded.

"Nah, my guess is he's far away from here, making another plan." He continued across the lot.

Her steps faltered at his remark. She hurried to catch up with him. "That was a bit brutal."

"True, but we shouldn't downplay what's happening."
He stopped next to Laura's blue sedan.

The front end had crumpled into the dashboard, and
the windows had shattered. Blood covered the airbag that
hung from the steering wheel like a deflated balloon, and
its white powder dusted the interior.

Cassidy gasped. She'd studied the pictures, but standing here—seeing her cousin's car up close—sent a shock
wave crashing into her. The report stated that Laura had
lived through the initial wreck. The fire department had
extracted her, but she'd died on the way to the hospital.
Had her cousin suffered in pain? Or had she died unaware?

"Don't go there, Cass."

She bristled. "Now you read minds?"

"It doesn't take a genius to know where your thoughts
had gone." Kyle laid a hand on her arm. "Rachel and Peter
were the paramedics that responded to the call. I talked
with them after it happened, and they said Laura never regained consciousness. I hope that helps."

Cassidy blinked back tears. "It does. At least a little."

Kyle placed the evidence kit on the ground and gestured
toward the car. "Shall we?"

She inhaled and pulled a pair of nitrile gloves from the
kit. "Come on."

"I propose we do this systematically. Start at the trunk
where there's no damage and work our way forward."

"Sounds good to me." She appreciated Kyle's thought-
fulness. Starting at the back bumper allowed her to gain
distance from the case and work it as a detective, not as
a family member.

He popped the trunk and handed her a flashlight.
"What's the old saying? No stone unturned?" He waggled his eyebrows.

"Just search the car, you goofball." She smiled. It felt

good to tease with Kyle again. Kind of like old times—yet not.

The two combed the car from the trunk to the back seat inch by inch. They snapped a few pictures, but beyond that, they found nothing new.

Kyle peered at her through the car. "Time to tackle the front seat and the mess the collision and the fire department made."

Cassidy stood and arched her back, stretching out the stiffness. "I've dreaded this part."

Hand on the top of the passenger door, his gaze met hers. His lopsided sad smile warmed her heart. "I know you have. Want to trade sides?"

She rubbed the back of her wrist under her nose, relieving an itch and debated his offer. "Stay where you are. I'll take the driver's seat."

"If you're sure."

Her determination wavered. She could do this—had to do it. "I think it'll help me mentally process what happened."

"Then, by all means. But if it becomes too much, say so, and I'll switch with you."

"I appreciate that." She tilted her head and studied him. "Why are you being so nice?"

His brows rose to his hairline. "Are you saying I shouldn't be?"

"No, no. It's just that you seem different."

"Chalk it up to a close call." His brown eyes softened. A wave of black hair dropped onto his forehead, and he brushed it back.

Her insides turned to jelly at the smile he flashed in her direction. The near death experiences had sparked an interest she hadn't expected. She'd always found him attractive but off-limits. Today... *Come on, Cassidy, give it a rest. For the love of everything, he was your best friend's fiancé.* Besides, he'd never want someone like her. He deserved a woman who fit his laidback personality. She was not that person.

She pushed the errant thought aside. The search awaited. She sucked in a breath and clicked on her flashlight.

Time to see if the car gave up any secrets.

Head tucked under the dashboard, Kyle moved his flashlight inch by inch over the floorboard. The cold seeped through the holes in his jeans, and the nitrile gloves gave little to no protection against the plummeting temps. He dreamed of a warm shower, a hot meal and another dose of ibuprofen. But he had a job to do, and he planned to give it his full attention for Cassidy's sake. Whether they proved her theory of a killer or not, she'd get the closure she deserved.

Cassidy had retreated into herself and hadn't said a word for the last twenty minutes since they moved to examine the front portion of the car.

The silence worried him. Although he didn't blame her. The reality of her cousin's life ending in the car had a sobering effect on him. He imagined it was ten times worse for Cassidy.

A circular stain like a doughnut on the passenger side carpet grabbed his attention. He reached for the file he'd placed in the evidence collection kit and flipped the pages until he located the photos of the inside of the car.

Cassidy popped her head up from the foot well of the driver's side. "Find something?"

"A round spot on the carpet. I'm trying to see if it belonged to a specific object taken into evidence." He studied each picture.

"Well?"

"Not that I can see." His mind whirled at the possible reasons for the mark. "Could be an old stain."

"Or it could be significant."

He held a photo next to the spot. "I don't see it in the picture."

"Why don't you collect a section of the carpet and take it to the lab rats."

His gaze jerked to her. "Lab rats?"

She shrugged. "When in Rome."

He laughed. "I promise not to tell them you said that." His shoulders relaxed, and his smile grew. She'd teased him a few times during the last couple of hours. This was the Cassidy he remembered.

Kyle snapped a picture of the stain, then cut a small square of the carpet and placed it in an evidence bag. "Done." After storing it in the kit, he opened the photo app on his phone. "Is that strange or what?"

Cassidy paused her search and squinted at the picture. "There's a solid circle in the middle of the stain that's the normal color of the floor."

"Weird, right?"

"Definitely." She tipped her head upside down to look under the front seat.

Kyle watched her for a moment.

The woman had taken several beatings, whether by the hands of the killer or his defensive reactions. And still, she brushed off the injuries that no doubt ached to prove her cousin hadn't died drinking and driving. Amber was right. Cassidy was driven to the point of putting everything aside, even her own well-being, to find the truth. He'd heard bits and pieces about her childhood, but she'd never divulged details. Her comments in the shop triggered a curiosity that refused to subside.

He clicked on his flashlight and continued his examination of the floor for any little fiber that appeared out of place. "What was up with the memory earlier?"

Cassidy jerked her head up and banged it on the steering wheel column. "Ouch." She rubbed the sore spot. "Why?"

"Chalk it up to getting to know you a little better."

"You really mean that?"

He shrugged. "I'd like to think we could be friends again." *Or more.* Wait. Where did that come from? He brushed the lingering thought aside.

She bit her lower lip. "I suppose." She looked iffy about his proposal but seemed to accept it. "I was thinking about my dad."

"Tell me about him. I know he died overseas during a deployment."

Cassidy sighed and returned to her search. "He was killed in action right after I turned eighteen. My mother died of cancer when I was twelve so it was just the two of us for six years. I stayed with our neighbor Meredith Horton, a retired teacher whose adult children lived out of town. She was like a grandmother to me."

"Was it hard to be away from your father?" Kyle moved his light to the passenger seat and continued his slow examination of the car.

"Actually, quite the opposite. I loved my dad, but the man demanded perfection." She got quiet for a moment, and he wondered if she'd finish her story.

She cleared her throat. "Mistakes were not allowed. So, when he deployed, I got a reprieve from the looks of disdain when I brought home an A on a test instead of an A plus."

"Wow. I had no idea." Unattainable expectations had to have been hard, and explained so much about her.

"Not many knew, and I don't go around advertising the fact."

"It all makes sense now."

"Excuse me?"

"Your OCD tendencies, your need to excel and your high personal standards for your work."

"Yeah, well, you grow up ashamed of yourself for not being perfect and see what it does to you." Her voice didn't hold the bite he'd expected, but something akin to sadness.

"I'm sorry for what you went through." And here, he'd blamed her for Amber's death. His words must have felt like a dagger in an open wound. He'd had no right to take out his guilt on her like that. He'd apologized for blaming her for Amber's death, but he needed to say more. It was time to man up and admit the truth about his past. "Cassidy, I—"

"What in the world?" She held a coin in the tweezers.

"What'd you find?"

"It's a quarter." She lifted it for him to see.

"O-kay. I don't understand the fascination."

"Look." She pointed to the year. "It might be nothing, but that's the same year Laura was born."

"Cassidy." She couldn't be serious. Finding change in a car, not an uncommon occurrence. But the hope in her blue eyes had him giving in. "I think you're stretching the find a bit, but bag it. We'll take it to the lab."

When they finished processing the car, Kyle returned the key to Ben and held the shop door open for Cassidy. "Let's get this stuff to the lab rats and call it a day."

"Sounds good to me."

He escorted Cassidy across the street, maintaining a constant scan of the area until they made it inside the truck. A glance in her direction tied his stomach in knots.

Teeth clenched and eyes glistening with unshed tears, Cassidy stared out the passenger window.

"What's wrong?"

"I promised my aunt and uncle that I'd keep Laura safe. I failed."

"Don't do that to yourself. You can't control everything."

She swiped a finger under her eye.

Her words about her father's demand for excellence rang in Kyle's ears. The woman strived to be the best, not because she wanted to, but because she had to.

How had he been so wrong about her?

TEN

The events of yesterday had caught up with Cassidy. Her insomnia had returned last night, and she hadn't fallen asleep until four in the morning.

Kyle had graciously allowed her to sleep in until he'd received a call from the sheriff asking them to come to the office for an afternoon update meeting.

The hum of the truck tires lulled her toward sleep. Between the late night and her injuries, she struggled to stay awake. The emotional impact of Laura's car added to her exhaustion. She guessed she suffered from a bit of depression as well.

She forced her eyes open and checked the mirrors for her assailant. The drone attack and attempted hit-and-run had put her on edge. She trusted Kyle, but she'd be negligent if she left her safety up to him.

"I'm thinking we hit a drive-thru for lunch." Kyle turned the heater on high.

Warm air flooded the inside of the vehicle. She held her cold fingers in front of the vents to thaw. The temperatures had dropped even further today.

"Food sounds good since I slept through breakfast." Her stomach growled on cue.

Kyle chuckled. "Lunch it is. By the way, I got a text message from Keith."

"Did he find something?"

"He didn't say. Just wanted to make sure he'd see us at the office." Kyle glanced at her and then back to the road.

Her shoulders drooped.

"Don't give up hope. We'll figure it out one way or the other. Either a serial killer is on the loose, or he's not. But once the guys gather the evidence and we go over it, we'll know how to proceed. And never fear, we are all determined to find the person targeting you."

"Thank you for that." Cassidy slouched in her seat. What did she have left in life? Her closest friends were gone. Her job hung in the balance, tipping toward disaster. And she waited on a decision on whether or not anyone believed her about the serial killer. People questioning her abilities was not an everyday occurrence. Her father's words had propelled her to be one of the best. She had no doubt he'd be disappointed in her right now—and at the moment, she agreed.

After a quick lunch in the truck, Kyle held the door open to the sheriff's department office.

"Thanks." She hurried inside.

"Good afternoon, you two." The lady at the front desk greeted them. "The others are waiting for you in the conference room."

"Thanks, Annie." Kyle placed his hand on the small of Cassidy's back and escorted her to the rear of the office.

Voices drifted into the hallway.

They entered the conference room, and the others said their hellos.

"Have a seat, Cassidy." Amy tapped the chair beside her. "I need reinforcements with all these men."

Cassidy smiled. She had a feeling from everything she'd learned about Amy that the woman could hold her own. "Glad to help."

"What did you all find?" Kyle scooted a chair back and eased onto the seat.

She took a long look at him. Dark circles stood out under his eyes. His stilted movements reminded her of the wounds he'd sustained. Well aware of her own injuries, Cassidy understood the soreness.

Amy dug in her purse and tossed a bottle of ibuprofen at Kyle. "Take that." She glanced at Cassidy. "You too."

"Yes, Mom." Kyle took the medicine and handed it to Cassidy.

"Thanks." She wouldn't argue. Her aches had aches.

Dennis rolled a pen between his hands. "As a favor to me, the lab rats worked through the night to get us preliminary answers. Melanie called and said she has news and will be here soon. But Amy's the one who called this meeting, so I'll turn it over to her."

"Thank you, Dennis." Amy spread several pictures on the table. "After examining the photographic evidence, I have a few questions. I've chosen three, but I have others that are similar."

"Which ones?" Keith asked his wife.

"The car accident where the driver lost control on a slick road, the home invasion and the mugging." Amy pointed to each one. "I'm sure the crime scene techs did a great job, but I look for different things."

"And?" Dennis leaned forward.

Amy grinned. "Patience, my friend."

"Amy," the sheriff scolded.

"I'm getting there." Amy flipped the image outward and touched the cap of her pen at a shadow on the edge of the photo. "That, my friends, is a footprint."

"Could it be one of the first responders?"

"Not unless they wore loafers. And here." Amy tapped the second photo. "See the ruts on the other side of the road, away from the accident? I'm curious as to who made those."

"And the mugging?" Dennis asked.

"That one is interesting. You can see a ripped piece of paper in the corner of the picture. I enlarged it. It's not conclusive, but it has a similar design to 4Gen Tech. But it's not enough to be certain." Amy leaned back and swung her chair back and forth.

Jason scowled. "Looks like part of a business card."

"That has potential." Doug jotted down a note on his pad of paper. "I'll take that one."

"Oh, I almost forgot. Doug sent me a still of the homeless guy who set off his security system the other night."

Cassidy jerked her gaze to Doug.

He shrugged. "I figured it wouldn't hurt to have Amy look at it."

"And I discovered that your culprit might have dressed in ratty clothes, but his shoes are of the expensive leather variety. Could be he found them, or someone donated them…" Amy let the statement hang.

"Or that guy's not homeless at all, only pretending to be." The creases in Kyle's forehead deepened. "I want to visit the guy Jason interviewed. The one who witnessed Sandy and Michael Hughes's carjacking. See if he recognizes anyone in the homeless community who might fit the description. I'll admit, I'm confused if the guy is guilty of the shooting or just at the wrong place at the wrong time. PD doesn't have enough evidence to make a definitive conclusion. But it's worth a shot to talk with him."

"I'll send you a copy of the picture," Doug said.

Amy scooped up the photos. "I know it's not much. You asked me to look for odd and out-of-place things. Without hours to study each photo in depth, this is what I found."

"Thanks, Amy. We appreciate it," Jason said.

"No problem. I have to go, but I'll keep looking." Amy patted her husband, Keith, on the top of the head and left the room.

"Well, what do y'all think?" Dennis asked.

"I'm the one pushing the serial killer theory, and I think it's slim." Cassidy hated to admit it, but flimsy was accurate.

"We keep looking. I'm not convinced, but I'm not ready to call it quits." Dennis's decision to continue to investigate surprised her.

Melanie rushed in, breathing hard. "Sorry that I'm late."

Jason hurried to her side. "Are you okay?"

"Walking is becoming more difficult without getting winded." Melanie took the seat that Jason offered.

Keith slid her a glass of water.

"Thanks." She took a sip.

"You said you had news. But take your time and catch your breath first." Dennis checked his watch. "We have time."

A moment later, Melanie exhaled. "That's better."

Jason sat beside her and stretched his arm across her shoulders. "Go ahead. We're listening."

"The lab rats pulled an all-nighter to do a preliminary examination of the piece of carpet Kyle submitted for analysis." She pinned Dennis with a playful glare. "Thanks for that, by the way. It's a good thing it's slow at work. They're not worth much today."

Dennis held his palms up. "I'll make it up to you."

"You better." Melanie returned her attention to the others. "Anyhoo, what they discovered was confusing, to say the least."

"So, it's inconclusive." Cassidy's shoulders slumped. She'd had such high hopes.

"I didn't say that." Melanie smiled. "We'll have to complete a full analysis, but the substance appears to have a mixture of alcohol, and what we can only conclude was dry ice."

"I don't understand," Kyle said.

"That's where the research comes into play since detecting dry ice is nearly impossible. I phoned a friend early this morning, which led me to a search for confirmation." Melanie shifted in her chair. "There, that's better. Have you ever heard of vaporized alcohol?"

Dennis's gaze narrowed. "I've heard of it but never seen it."

"Neither had I…until now. It explains the lack of alcohol in Laura's stomach content."

Cassidy sat forward. "How does that work?"

"There are several methods, but I think the most likely is that someone used dry ice to vaporize the alcohol and forced your cousin Laura to breathe it in. It's not only dangerous but deadly."

"How would they make her inhale it?" Jason asked.

"That I can't answer. But all it takes is getting the vapors into someone's nose and mouth."

Tears burned Cassidy's eyes. "It wasn't a drunk driving accident." She'd believed it all along, but hearing another explanation sent a wave of relief through her.

"I reviewed the autopsy report and discussed it with Dr. Wade, the medical examiner. It's my professional opinion that Laura died from complications due to vaporized alcohol. It's highly unlikely she did this to herself, and Dr. Wade has made the appropriate notations in the document. We can't officially make the determination, but it explains the BAL and the lack of alcohol in her stomach."

Kyle rested his hand on hers. "I'm sorry I doubted you about Laura."

His apology meant a lot, but the warmth in his eyes sent butterflies loose in her stomach.

"I don't know, guys. She was right about this, maybe she is right about the other victims too. I'm willing to keep digging. What do you think?" Kyle's gaze landed on each member of the team.

Doug tossed his pen on the table. "I'm in."

"Me too," Keith said, followed by Jason's agreement.

Kyle shifted to face Cassidy. "Are you ready to prove the rest of your theory?" He smiled. His dimples showed, giving him a youthful look.

Her muscles turned to jelly with relief. They hadn't given up on her yet.

She nodded, not confident her voice wouldn't give away the effect Kyle had on her sanity.

ELEVEN

Kyle lowered his achy body from the truck. He and Cassidy both needed another day to rest and recover, but he didn't blame her for wanting to press on.

As soon as Dennis dismissed the team, the two of them agreed to interview the homeless man who'd talked with Jason. The dress shoes had piqued Kyle's interest, and he wanted answers.

He turned to Cassidy. "How are you feeling?"

"About as good as you." Her shy grin made him smile. "That good, eh?"

She laughed, and it sounded wonderful.

He'd missed the softer side of her. "You need to do that more often."

She scrunched her forehead. "Do what?"

"Laugh."

"There hasn't been a lot of reason to do that lately."

He understood. "Maybe we can spend more time together once you're safe."

"I'd like that. You used to come around anytime you were off duty. I've missed you."

His heart leaped at her admission.

"Then it's a plan." He parked the rental truck and motioned to their destination. "Come on, let's find our witness."

Jason had stated that the man had sobered up and had found a part-time job but still lived on the streets, using the shelter to shower before his shifts.

The stench that filled the alley known for the Valley Springs homeless population made Kyle flinch.

The sheriff's department came to the alley often to bring food and support those who lived there. He'd never seen it so neglected or deserted since he started visiting when he'd moved into town.

The folks who called the area home cared for each other and kept the space free of unsanitary habits.

What had happened?

He stood, hands on his hips, and scanned the tents, cardboard boxes, shopping carts and sleeping bags. Not one person lingered nearby.

Cassidy stepped next to him. "This is too quiet."

"I agree. Maybe the shelter picked everyone up for a hot meal and an offer to stay inside. The weather *is* getting colder." But he'd never seen the place abandoned.

"Is this normal?"

He shook his head. "Not at all. I'd like to look around. See if we can find anyone."

"I'm good with that. I'd like to ask a few questions myself."

Every tent and box was empty as they moved toward the end of the alley. "This is just weird."

"Over there." Cassidy pointed to what looked like feet sticking out from beneath a stack of cardboard. "Is that a pair of dress shoes?"

Kyle squinted. "It looks like it." He motioned for her to follow. Approaching unannounced wasn't a good idea, so he called out, "Excuse me. Sir, are you awake?"

The person didn't move.

He tried again. "Sir, can you hear me?"

"Is he alive?" Cassidy leaned to the side, peering at the shoes.

"Unfortunately, he's probably drunk. Be careful. We don't want to startle him and elicit a negative reaction."

She rolled her eyes. "I'm not a rookie. I've dealt with my fair share of questionable situations."

"Point taken." Kyle continued toward the goal.

Cassidy grabbed him, threw him backward and off to the side. He hit the brick wall and slid down.

She appeared in his line of sight. "Get down!"

Kyle glanced up in time to watch a piece of PVC pipe roll toward a wire. His eyes widened. A trip wire. He threw his body over Cassidy.

An explosion filled the air, sending debris flying.

The rubble peppered his back.

He held Cassidy close, praying they both survived.

Cassidy's ears rang. Her cheek, plastered to the asphalt, ached. Smoke and dust swirled around her, making it impossible to see beyond a few feet in front of her. She coughed, but the weight on top of her kept her from getting a full breath.

Heat warmed her skin. The raid. The explosion. Her team. Her arms burned, and sweat beaded on her upper lip.

"Cass?"

Her mind struggled to catch up with what had happened. Not the raid, but the alleyway. Kyle's foot, six inches from the trip wire. She almost hadn't seen it.

Thank You, God.

Nausea swirled in her belly. She'd come close to failing another person in her life.

"Cassidy?" Kyle's tone sharpened.

"I'm here. But something's on top of me." Heat wafted in her direction. Face pinned away from the explosion, being unable to see the flames scared her more than she cared to admit.

"That would be me."

"Can you move so I can breathe?" The weight shifted, and she filled her lungs for the first time since the blast. "Thanks. Are you hurt?" Cassidy rolled over and got a good look at the dying flames. Her pulse slowed.

Kyle grabbed her hand and tugged her away from the fire. At the end of the alley, he pressed his back against the brick wall, slid to the ground and closed his eyes. "I have a few more bruises and scratches to add to my collection. That was a little too close for my taste."

She sat next to him. "I don't recommend doing it again."

His gaze met hers. "Are you really okay?"

"Nothing time won't fix."

"What about flashbacks from the raid?"

She shrugged. "I already have them occasionally—what's a few more."

"Stop that. Stop downplaying your feelings."

"What do you want me to say? I'm scared. My hands are shaking. I want to throw up. I'm struggling to keep my mind from reliving the explosions over and over. Well, they're all true." Rivulets of tears poured down her cheeks. "I'm not the perfect all-together person everyone wants me to be."

Kyle wrapped his arms around her and pulled her close. "You don't have to be perfect. Just be you."

She laid her head on his chest. Her body shook like a nervous Chihuahua, and the tears refused to stop falling.

"I've got you." Kyle rubbed her back. "We're okay, thanks to you."

Several minutes later, she pulled away and instantly missed the warmth of his embrace. "I'm sorry that I got you all wet." She wiped the front of his jacket.

"I'll dry." He tipped up her chin. "Feel better?"

She chuckled. "Yeah, I do."

"Good." He hesitated a moment, retrieved his phone from his pocket and placed a call.

"Nine-one-one, what's your emergency?"

"Sonja, this is Detective Howard. There was an explosion at the homeless camp. I need fire and a crime scene crew."

"Copy that." He heard Sonja relaying the message. "Do you need medical?"

"It's not urgent. Only scrapes and bruises."

"Everyone's on the way. And heads up, the sheriff went code three out of here when he heard."

"Copy that." Kyle hung up. Wonderful. His boss left the office with lights and sirens. "Brace yourself. You're about to see the mother hen side of Dennis."

She laughed. "Now that's a picture I'll never get out of my mind."

Cassidy pressed her hand on the wall and stood. She turned and got her first good look at the damage. "Wow. Talk about targeted. That was meant for whoever tripped the wire. There's no other damage. And check it out. The box at the end of the alley moved. No one is there. Only the shoes."

"So, it was a setup all along. Ever get the feeling someone's out to get us?" Kyle crossed his arms over his chest and winced at the tug of the new scrapes on his back.

"Who knew we were coming here?"

"Only the team. And they had no reason to tell anyone."

"How is he finding us? Or should I say me?" She felt like a cat with nine lives. Only, she'd used eight of them.

The flash of lights and whine of sirens filled the air. Multiple vehicles raced in their direction.

"Looks like Sonja called the entire town."

"Sonja?"

"Our dispatcher."

Cassidy inhaled and braced herself for the barrage of questions from the fire department, PD and sheriff's department. Technically, VSPD had jurisdiction, but she doubted the sheriff would stand aside without a fight.

An Anderson County Sheriff's Department SUV hit the brakes, and the sheriff threw open the door and strode toward them. "What happened?"

She and Kyle walked Dennis through the events, including spotting the trip wire at the last second.

"You two need to see the medics." Dennis's suggestion held the tone of an order.

"Sheriff." Doug rushed over. "I just spotted John Morrison driving away from the area."

"What was he doing here?" Kyle asked.

"No idea. But he drove in the direction of his office when I arrived on the scene."

Dennis pointed to her and Kyle. "You two get cleaned up and get some rest. Doug, I want you to visit Mr. Morrison. Don't make assumptions. I want him interviewed again."

"No." Kyle planted himself in front of Dennis. "Sheriff Monroe, I want to look the guy in the face when he explains why he was in the area."

The use of his title paused Dennis's response.

"I need to find out who tried to kill us." Kyle refused to back down, but the request was personal. "Come on, Dennis. Let me do this."

Dennis stared him down. "No careless action. No retaliation. Get the information and report back."

"On it, boss." Kyle grasped Cassidy's arm and gently tugged her to the truck. "Let's get out of here before the paramedics zero in on us."

"I'm with you on that one." She jumped into the rental truck and scanned the street.

Was John Morrison her attacker, or was a killer out there—watching—planning his next move?

Kyle refused to change his clothes before confronting John Morrison, but he and Cassidy had taken time to treat the new scrapes acquired from the explosion.

Anger simmered, and he struggled to keep it from boiling over. If Morrison had anything to do with the trip wire that targeted Cassidy, Kyle would make sure the man paid for his action.

He held the door open for her at Morrison's office building, and the two of them marched to the receptionist's desk.

Khloe stopped typing on her computer and met his gaze. "May I help you, Detectives?"

Good. She remembered him. "We need to speak with Mr. Morrison."

"I'm sorry, but he can't be interrupted at the moment."

Kyle inhaled and released the breath. *Stay calm.* "Khloe, there are questions I need answered, and your boss is the only one who can do that. Now, please tell him we must speak with him."

The young woman seemed to understand that his patience had waned. "I'll do what I can." Khloe hurried down the hall.

"I think you scared her." Cassidy toyed with the bandages on her hand.

"I'm not in the mood to be messed with. You could have died today."

"Same for you, Kyle."

The click of heels signaled Khloe's return. "Mr. Morrison said he'd see you now, but he has a meeting in ten minutes that he can't miss."

"Fine."

"Follow me, please."

Kyle placed his hand on the small of Cassidy's back and trailed behind Khloe.

The receptionist opened the office door and invited them inside.

Morrison stood behind his large oak desk. "Detectives, I don't have much time, but how can I help you?"

Cassidy joined Kyle in front of John Morrison. "We have a few questions for you."

The tech guru folded his arms across his chest. "I'll do my best to answer."

Kyle made a note of the man's closed-off stance. "Where were you an hour ago?"

Morrison's flinch was so subtle that most people would have missed it. "I've had meetings all day. I did go next door for a cup of coffee, but other than that, I haven't left the office."

Cassidy opened her mouth, but Kyle shook his head. He didn't want to alert Morrison that they caught him in a lie. He had gone farther than to the coffee shop.

She pursed her lips, not liking that he'd stopped her. Her spine straightened. "Mr. Morrison, why didn't you tell us that the carjacking you witnessed was that of your business partners?"

Anger flashed in the man's eyes, but his voice remained neutral. "Witnessing the shooting isn't something I want to think about. I hope you understand."

The man was daft if he thought Kyle would let it go that easily. "What was your relationship with the Hugheses? How well did you get along?"

"I don't like what you implied, detective. Do I need a lawyer?"

"Not at all. I only asked a question."

Morrison's jaw twitched. "I think your time is up. If you'll excuse me, I have a meeting to conduct. You know the way out."

"We'll go for now, but if we have more questions for you, we'll be back." Kyle jutted his head toward the door.

Cassidy took the hint and exited the office. She started to say something.

"Not yet. Wait until we get outside."

They strode from the office building and headed to the rental truck. "What were you going to say?"

"Did you see the framed business logo with the four quarters?"

"No. I was too focused on Morrison. Why?"

"4Gen Tech. As in 4 Geniuses. How arrogant can he be?"

"I wondered what it stood for." Kyle unlocked the truck, and they got in.

"I can't believe he flat-out lied to us about his whereabouts when the explosion happened. Yes, he admitted he left the office, but only went next door. Why would he do that unless he had something to hide?"

"I don't know, but let's report back to Dennis and see what he thinks. It's flimsy for a warrant, but you never know. Besides, the sheriff is good with stuff like that." He placed the call. Once he hung up, Kyle pulled from the parking lot. "Dennis said he'd try. He'll let us know in the morning."

Cassidy slouched in the seat. "I hate the wait."

"Me too, but we don't have much of a choice. Let's get some sleep, so we're ready for tomorrow."

He glanced at her and noted the bags under her eyes. They both needed time to rest and recover.

Cassidy returned to Doug's house, refused dinner and took a hot shower to wash off the grime from her eventful day.

Comfortable in sweatpants and a sweatshirt, she collapsed on the bed. Her body hurt, and her head ached. She'd downed a couple tablets of ibuprofen and craved sleep. The concerned look in Kyle's eyes had unraveled her composure. She'd escaped before she'd fallen apart in front of him and Doug.

Tears flowed unchecked. She'd never survive if she lost another person she cared about. And Kyle had come six inches from meeting Jesus face-to-face.

She closed her eyes. Praying the images disappeared.

Cassidy's heart pounded. The wire stretched tight a couple of feet in front of her. A scream caught in her throat. She had to stop Kyle...

Amber's eyes widened, causing Cassidy to peer inside the side window next to the front door. Red numbers on a timer counted down. The digits glowed six, five... She had to stop her team...

Kyle's foot landed inches from the thin line, waiting to blow him up. She grabbed his arm and yanked him away from the trip wire...

Cassidy had to stop her team. She fisted her hand in the air, but would it be in time? Amber met her gaze a second before her friend shouldered McCarthy out of the way and breached the door...

Boom! The explosion threw Cassidy across the lawn.

Her eyes flew open. Nausea swirled in her belly. She stumbled to the ensuite bathroom and retched. Two nightmares had intertwined, switching back and forth in rapid succession, leaving her no way of discerning where one ended and the other began.

Another wave of the memories hit her in full color, and a cry escaped. Amber had breached early, sacrificing herself to save the team. Three more seconds and the task force would have been in place, and more people would have died. Instead, they'd had serious injuries but the only fatality was Amber.

Cassidy sat, leaning against the wall, and rested her head on her knees. Sobs racked her body, and sweat matted her hair. *Oh, Amber.*

"Cass?"

She lifted her face and found Kyle kneeling next to her.

"I heard you getting sick. I called out, but you didn't answer. I'm sorry for barging in, but I couldn't stay away."

Tears flowed unchecked down her cheeks.

"Honey, what's wrong? Did the explosion today trigger a nightmare?"

It was so much more than that, but speaking was beyond her abilities, so she nodded.

Kyle sat next to her and tugged her close.

She buried her face in his chest and cried for her friend who'd made the ultimate sacrifice.

TWELVE

The morning sun reflected off the street-level windows of the sheriff's office, sending a glare into Cassidy's eyes, which stung from her crying jag last night.

A bit mortified that Kyle had found her on the floor in that state, she'd let him hold her until the tears subsided. A gesture that soothed her battered heart.

This morning, they'd both admitted to a restless night's sleep, leaving them irritable and short-tempered. But she had a killer to stop, so she pressed on.

She and Kyle had arrived at the sheriff's department office ten minutes ago, prepared to serve the warrant to Morrison as soon as Sheriff Monroe secured it. She paced a six-foot section of the sidewalk. The memories she'd lived through last night made her edgy, and if the judge didn't come through…her nerves might snap.

Justice. That's what she wanted for all the victims she'd identified, along with her cousin. A look into the man's office and home could give her the evidence she needed. She just had to get into both—legally. "We're wasting time! We need that warrant!"

Cell phone to his ear, Kyle held up his hand, cutting her off. "Yes, but at the interview… No, sir… But… All right, I'll tell her." He pressed the end button and sighed. "No go on the warrant."

"Why not?" She clenched her hands. "Morrison lied. He'll cover his tracks, and we'll never stop him."

"First of all, you don't know for sure it's him. He might have had another reason for being near the alleyway yesterday, like stepping out on his wife." The bruises on Kyle's face had deepened to a dark purple. He'd snipped at her several times this morning, but she'd ignored it. The man looked ready to drop.

Her own fatigue and frustration bested her. She threw her hands in the air. "If we had the warrant, we'd have the evidence."

"Getting a warrant means we get to search his stuff, but it guarantees nothing. We have no motive. We have no sense of opportunity. We have virtually nothing except a whiff of suspicion. For all we know, this could be a dead end we end up wasting time on."

"What?" she asked, stunned at his outburst.

"You're being reckless." Kyle fisted his hands. "You're not going about this rationally and carefully! We have Morrison's connection to some of the victims, but not to your cousin or to others. You're rushing into this. That can lead to risk, and haven't we faced enough of that already as a team? Maybe Amber would be alive if you'd taken a moment to think logically!" His voice skyrocketed with each word.

She stopped and stared at him. They both ran on fumes right now, but he'd hit a nerve. "That's where you're going with this? You're never going to get past your anger to see the truth, are you?"

"And what's that, Cassidy?" He stepped in front of her and crossed his arms. The challenge in his eyes had her sucking in a breath. "You don't remember. So, we'll never know."

"But I do," she whispered. The memory had sent her to her knees last night. Probably why her whole body buzzed with fury. The flashbacks had hit hard when she'd gone to bed. The details she'd never remembered had come in full color. But she hadn't been able to tell him while he comforted her. And when she woke up this morning, she'd chosen to wait until they found the killer before she sat down with him to reveal the truth. For her sake and his.

"You…" The blood drained from his face. He took her by the arm and pulled her to the truck. "Let's go."

She complied and slipped into the passenger seat. Why hadn't she told him the minute her memory came back? She planned to give him the details of what happened, but this was not how she wanted it to go down.

Kyle cranked the engine and took off. Several blocks later, on a quiet street, he pulled over. He shifted in his seat and draped his left hand over the steering wheel. His eyes filled with agony. "Last night?"

Cassidy nodded.

"I sat with you for an hour, holding you in my arms. Why didn't you say anything?"

"I'm still dealing with the memory myself. I needed time, and I didn't want a rushed conversation."

"I think it's time you spit it out."

She flinched at the bite in his words. "Fine." Her heart raced at the recollection, and sweat beaded on her forehead. "Yesterday, after our close call with the trip wire, memories of the raid came back in flashes. For the first time since the explosion, my nightmares revealed the truth."

He stared at her, not saying a word.

The silence set her nerves on edge.

Tears trailed down her cheeks. Cassidy forced the words from her mouth. "She breached early on purpose."

"What? Why?" Kyle looked like someone had punched him in the gut.

"The guys were moving into position, and I prepared

to start the countdown once everyone was in place. I saw Amber lean in as if she saw something in the little side window. That's when I noticed it too. The drug dealer had rigged the door to blow. The timer only had seconds left. Amber pushed McCarthy out of the way and breached before the team got too close." Cassidy choked back a sob. "She sacrificed herself to save us. Sure, we had injuries." She lifted her hand and made a fist, stretching the burn scars that ran down her forearm. "But no one was killed—except for Amber. We owe her our lives."

Tears streamed down Kyle's cheeks. "So, she's a hero?"

"Yes. And now that I remember, I'll make sure my boss knows." Cassidy regretted not forcing herself to remember until now. Then again, yesterday might have jarred it loose.

Kyle nodded and closed his eyes. Pain etched his features, making her want to reach out to him, but she thought better of it.

How would Kyle respond? Would he blame himself like he did before? "It's not your fault, you know. Your argument had nothing to do with her choice."

Kyle straightened in his seat and put the truck into Drive. "I'll drop you off with Doug."

"Kyle. Don't do this. Talk to me."

"I'm not as sure as you are that my actions didn't play a role in her death." He rubbed the back of his neck and huffed. "I need time, Cassidy. Please don't fight me on that." His tone told her not to argue.

As he drove to Doug's, she watched the houses go by, wondering if she'd made things better or worse by telling Kyle the truth.

Kyle dropped off Cassidy, confirmed Doug had her secure inside the house and left. His mind struggled to grasp what Cassidy had revealed.

The Christmas decorations in the yards pulled him deeper into his pain. He'd let a moment of weakness cloud his judgment and demanded that Amber make a choice about her job and children. Later that day, she'd died, and now he lived with the guilt of the ultimatum he'd given her.

"Why, Amber?" Kyle's eyes burned. "Did I push you to it?" His questions hung in the air.

His final, hateful words to his parents came to his mind. He'd take them back to have one more day with them. The stupid conversation played over and over in his dreams on a nightly basis.

He smacked the steering wheel. When would he learn to quit spouting off without thinking of the consequences?

If only his grandmother's health had allowed him to seek her wisdom, but in her condition, he refused to add a layer of stress.

On autopilot, Kyle pulled into the retirement community and parked in front of Judith Evans's apartment. The town grandmother and all-around dynamo, known for her straight-shooting advice, was just the person he needed. Someone to help him work through the new information about Amber sacrificing herself for her team.

His boots hit the ground, and the cold air stung his cheeks. Inhaling, he trudged up the sidewalk and knocked on the door. Judith's colorful wreath stared back at him. Christmas approached at a rapid speed, and he wasn't ready for the heartache of the day.

In his youth, the season had always been a time of hope, but tragic events had turned it into a depressing black hole of sorrow. Which made it worse. His heart pulled in two directions. Celebration and grief. The day meant for rejoicing, clouded by tragedy.

The door opened, and the spunky older woman stood before him in a hot pink sweatsuit. "Well, look who we have here. Come on in, Detective. You're just in time to arrest Harold for stealing cookies."

A smile tugged at his lip at the mention of her boyfriend. If anyone could pull him out of his funk, Judith fit the bill with her silliness.

"Sorry, ma'am, but I'm not here to investigate a cookie thief," Kyle said in his most formal tone.

She swatted at him. "Oh, you. Come in out of the cold and tell me why you're really here."

"Thanks." He entered, removed his boots and coat, and took a seat on the couch. Hands between his knees, he leaned forward. His shoulders drooped. The small reprieve from reality came and went. Pain and sorrow had returned.

Judith sat in her favorite recliner and raised a brow. "Better get it out, Kyle, before that frown becomes permanent."

"I'm confused, Miss Judith." How did he admit what he did?

"Does this have something to do with that sweet girl you've been protecting?"

Kyle jolted at her question. "Where did you hear that?"

"Pssh. Word travels fast around here." She tapped her manicured nail on the arm of the chair. "You expect me not to have informants when it comes to my boys?"

The woman had dubbed the four detectives and the sheriff as her boys, and they loved her for it. "I suppose you already know why I'm here then."

She chuckled. "How about you quit stalling and tell me what's wrong?"

"Leave it to you to get to the point." He forced a smile. He trusted Judith with his deepest, darkest secrets but the idea of telling her sent the acid in his stomach churning. Kyle wiped a hand down his face. "It seems like I have a habit of saying awful things to those I care about right before they die."

"Your parents and Amber?"

"Yes, ma'am." He closed his eyes. "That's not all, though." His gaze connected with Judith's.

"Go on. I'm listening." Her reassurance gave him the courage to continue.

"Several years ago, before I came to Valley Springs, my partner died in a needless accident."

Judith tapped her lower lip. "And you said something to him."

Kyle nodded.

"And you think your words killed all of them." Judith hadn't asked. She'd declared what his heart had shouted at him.

"Yes."

"What did you say that has tied you in knots?" She settled into her seat and gave him her full attention.

Kyle sighed. Might as well rip the Band-Aid off and get it over with. "My mom and dad refused to let me go to a party. I yelled that I hated them and walked out the door. They came searching for me when I didn't return, and a few hours later, they were dead."

Now that the words flowed, he couldn't stop. "Then, a few years ago, my partner ditched his wife and kids for a weekend with the guys. His daughter had an emergency appendectomy the day before, and he left his wife alone to care for his little girl and his six-month-old son. I told him he didn't appreciate his wife and kids and didn't deserve to be a father." Kyle wiped a hand down his face. "He stormed out of the office and got in his cruiser. He went faster than he should on the icy roads and crashed his vehicle. He died on impact."

"I see."

Then he told her the panicked ultimatum he'd given Amber, followed by her demise. "What if my words caused all of them to lose focus, and that's the reason they died? Or worse. What if Amber did it on purpose because of me?"

Judith pinned him with a hard look. "Oh, my dear boy, as much as I love you, you aren't that powerful."

He opened his mouth to respond.

"No, no." She waggled a finger. "You let God be God. Only He has the power of life and death. You must trust Him. You may not get the answers you want, and the outcomes might hurt, but He'll be there to comfort you. Nothing is beyond His ability."

"I've talked to God, asked Him to forgive me. But I still feel like it was my fault that they died. I should never have said those things."

"Sometimes it's harder to forgive ourselves even after we've asked for forgiveness from others. Maybe you should ask God to help you forgive yourself."

He hadn't thought about that. Maybe that was his problem. But he couldn't let go of what he'd said to Cassidy. "Judith, I hear what you're saying, but I went spouting off to Cassidy before I came here." He dropped his face into his hands. "What if something happens to her?"

Judith moved next to him and placed her hand on his shoulder. "Kyle, your words can't kill, but make no mistake, they *can* do damage." She rubbed circles on his back. "You care about her, don't you?"

"It's complicated."

"I don't think so. You either do or don't."

"But what about Amber?"

"Honey, she's gone. And believe me, she'd want you to be happy." Judith eased back against the cushions.

Did he care about Cassidy as more than a friend? He

couldn't deny that his heart did funny things around her. "I've said awful things to her. And don't forget that she was Amber's best friend."

Judith rested her hand on his arm. "Who better to understand and accept your memories of Amber? I haven't met the girl yet, but from what our sheriff told me, she's a wonderful woman."

"That she is." He'd be a fool to disagree. Did he want more with Cassidy? "You think she'd understand?"

"You were her best friend's fiancé. You both loved Amber. Why deny that? I'd guess she'd share a few memories of her own with you." Judith gave him a sad smile. "Look at Harold and me. I was married to his best friend. We don't deny ourselves the memories of my late husband. We embrace them. There's no jealousy involved. Only understanding and acceptance."

Kyle placed his hand over hers. "You're a wise woman, Miss Judith."

"And don't you forget it." She laughed. "Now, what are you going to do about this Cassidy woman?"

"I guess I better go have a chat with her before the Valley Springs grapevine gets to her." For the first time since Cassidy's bombshell, he felt lighter.

Judith swatted at him. "Get out of here and go get your girl."

He shook his head and put on his boots and coat. Cassidy wasn't his—not yet, anyway.

"You're a gem, Miss Judith." He placed a kiss on the older woman's cheek.

He jogged to the truck and headed to Doug's before he lost his nerve.

God, I know we haven't had a long talk in a while, and I apologize for that. But would you give me the courage to face Cassidy and tell her how I feel?

THIRTEEN

Unsure what to do with herself, Cassidy moved to the Christmas tree and placed her fingers under the glowing lights. She owed Amber her life. The whole team did. She wished she'd remembered months ago.

After Kyle dropped her off at Doug's, she'd placed a call to her boss, giving him the details of those missing moments in her report. He thanked her and asked how she was feeling. In the end, there was no offer to let her return to work. But to be honest, she was glad. It gave her more time to find her cousin's killer.

She wrapped her arms around her waist and stared at the flames dancing in the fireplace a few feet away.

How had she ended up here? Confused. Alone. And in love with her dead best friend's fiancé.

"What do I do, Amber?" she whispered.

"Cassidy?"

She spun to find Kyle watching her. "Hi." The timidity in her voice shocked her. But the man standing before her had her off balance. Did he hate her? Not trust her? Or had he felt the attraction between them? "Are you okay?"

Two strides, and he stood before her. "I'm sorry I overreacted. I've been horrible to you. Please forgive me."

"Forgive you? I'm the one who should be asking."

He shook his head. "I knew from the beginning that Amber's death wasn't your fault, but my guilt blinded me to the truth. I had to blame someone, and you were there."

"I was a coward. I hadn't wanted to face the pain to discover what had happened. I wish I'd been braver. You deserved to know the truth." She held up her hand, exposing the burn scars. "But I feared reliving the pain."

"I'm sorry you suffered, and I turned my back on you. My insecurities got in the way." Kyle traced a finger over the ridges on her arm.

Cassidy resisted the urge to pull away. No one had touched her scars—not in a loving manner, anyway. "Can we say we both made mistakes and leave it at that?"

"I think that's a great idea." He tucked a stray hair behind her ear. "I'm not sure what's going on between us."

Her heart thundered in her chest. Was he going to kiss her? "Me either."

"But I think I want to find out." He leaned in.

If she rose up on her toes, their lips would meet. Did she want that? Who was she kidding? "Kyle," she whispered on a ragged breath.

He tilted his head and closed the gap.

"Hey, Kyle? The sheriff and the crew are on the way over." Doug's voice came out of nowhere.

She jerked back and turned away. Her cheeks flamed with heat.

"Oops. Sorry. I'll just be in the kitchen." Doug hurried from the room.

"My partner has lousy timing," Kyle grumbled.

"No reason to shed blood." Cassidy left him standing there and moved to the couch. She forced her pulse to slow. "Let's get back to the cases and see if we can find the evidence for a search warrant."

"Doug's going to pay for that," Kyle muttered.

Cassidy bit her lip to hide her smile. At least she wasn't the only one frustrated at his partner's abrupt entrance.

She'd flown away from his touch and put distance between them. Afraid of her own traitorous heart. Could she open up to him? Kyle had taken a risk and been vulnerable with her. Should she do the same and admit her feelings?

"Kyle... I—"

The doorbell rang.

Kyle threw his hands in the air and huffed. "You'd think this is Grand Central Station." He headed for the door and let the others in.

Maybe now wasn't the time to confess that she cared about him as more than a friend. They both needed to heal before they tackled that Gordian knot.

The lost moment would be forever imprinted in Kyle's memory. He hadn't declared his feelings for her, but if she hadn't figured it out, her detective skills required work. Somewhere between the failed hit-and-run and the explosion, he'd lost his heart to her.

"Yo, Kyle." Jason tossed a wadded-up napkin at him. "Did you hear a word I said?"

The living room grew quiet, waiting for him to answer Jason's question. He had no idea what his friend had asked. He had to get his mind focused and away from Cassidy's kissable lips. "Sorry."

"That's what I thought. I said I think we've found something. From our interviews of the other cases and Doug's amazing computer skills, we've discovered that each of the victims has a commonality."

Cassidy straightened. "You found a connection?"

"Not exactly. But each victim had a power position in his or her company. The companies ranged from medium-size businesses to large corporations, but each person held an influential role. CEO, CFO, owner, on the board of directors. You get the picture."

Kyle mulled over the information. "That fits with the details that Doug found for our cases too. John, Sandy, Michael and Aaron started the computer company together, and all died except Mr. Morrison."

"Which makes me wonder why the killer didn't come after John again." Cassidy twirled a piece of hair around her finger.

"Unless he is the killer and staged his hit-and-run to make him look like a victim."

Dennis stood and paced the room. "It's still not enough evidence to get a warrant. But I'll admit, it makes me curious why he survived, and the others didn't."

The front door opened, and Amy waltzed in. She kissed Keith and plopped down on the floor. "Hi, everyone."

Doug stood. "I can get you a chair."

"Nah." Amy waved him off.

Keith ran his fingers through the end of his wife's hair. "Not that I'm not happy to see you, but what's up?"

Amy tilted her head back and smiled at her husband.

"Ugh." Jason made gagging noises.

"Oh, please. You and Melanie are worse than we are," Amy scolded. "Now, if you let me get to the point, I have a grandpa that needs saving from an active little boy."

Dennis returned to his seat. "Go ahead, Amy."

"You know that I've spotted inconsistencies in all crime scene photos. That the cases that the reporting officers deemed accidents are homicides. It's the homicides that we haven't been able to find a thread to link them."

"That about sums it up," Kyle said.

"Well, I'm here with that connection."

The room grew quiet. All eyes shifted to Amy. She

reached for a grape from the tray of snacks that Doug had supplied and popped it in her mouth.

Keith massaged her shoulders. "Ames, if you don't finish your explanation, I think boss man over there is going to blow a gasket waiting for you to get to the point."

"Sorry, Dennis."

The sheriff closed his eyes and shook his head. "It's okay, Amy. But if you'd please continue, I'd be grateful."

Amy removed several photos from the file she'd carried in. "If you look closely at each of these images, you'll see a coin. I've circled it with a wax pencil."

When the photographic evidence reached Kyle, he shared it with Cassidy.

She studied the picture. Her breath hitched. "There was a coin in Laura's car."

Kyle had forgotten all about the quarter. "Cassidy found it under the driver's seat." He fished his phone from his pocket and pulled up the picture he'd taken. "Here." He passed it around the room.

"The thing I noticed about the quarter is that the year on it was the same as Laura's birth year. I'm not sure why, but it struck me as unusual," Cassidy said.

"Amy?" Dennis urged her to check the dates.

"I'm on it." She grabbed her laptop and opened the crime scene files. "I enlarged the coins. Let me see if I can read the dates."

Doug opened his computer. "Give me the victim and the coin year, and I'll confirm our suspicions."

"First one, Sandy and Michael Hughes." Amy tilted her head and squinted at the screen. "Got it." She gave Doug the year.

The clicking of keys on the keyboard filled the room. "It's not a match to either birthday."

Cassidy sat up straight. "But it matches the year they founded the company."

"That's interesting. Keep going." Dennis leaned forward, his attention on Amy.

Amy rattled off the next set, then the next.

"Most of the cases have coins with matching birth years, and those that don't, the date matches the year the victim died. And the coin for the Hugheses is a match to the start of the company. The photos of the other crime scenes didn't show coins, but I wouldn't rule it out. Some of the files had minimal evidence collected due to the circumstances."

Dennis handed the pictures to Keith, who collected them for his wife. "Thanks, Amy."

"I'd say anytime, but you'd take me up on it. I'll see you all later." Amy smiled and let herself out.

Jason clapped his hands. "Now, we're getting somewhere."

Cassidy's eyes scanned the room. "So, you all believe me?"

Kyle clasped her fingers in silent support. He knew he believed her, but he waited for the others to give their opinions.

"I think I can speak for everyone here. I'm convinced there's a *possibility* of a serial killer, and I plan to reopen these cases," Dennis said.

The others agreed.

"I don't know what to say." Cassidy sat stunned, looking from one person to the next. She knew they'd doubted this theory from the get-go, but they'd stuck with her, respecting her abilities as an investigator, letting the evidence lead them. Now they were on board with the idea a serial killer could be responsible. She warmed with appreciation for this crew.

"How about let's get to work?" Jason teased.

Cassidy's smile bloomed.

"Jason, do you have anything for us about the attempts on Cassidy's life?" Dennis asked.

"Not much. I checked the camera at Ben's. No go on the license plate of the SUV that tried to run her over. A mud-like substance covered it. And there's no evidence at any of the scenes that indicated who has her in his sights," Jason said.

"What about the drone?" Kyle hadn't known that Dennis had tagged Jason to investigate the attacks on Cassidy.

"The techs are still working on it, but nothing as of yet." Jason sighed.

"If I'm right, it's the serial killer who's after me." Cassidy stared at Kyle as if asking him to back her up.

Kyle agreed with her to a point. "Since we are leaning toward a serial killer, let's confirm or disprove that theory then go from there."

"Let's do it." Keith rubbed his hands together. "So, what's up with the coins?"

Doug scratched his jaw. A habit the man had when he was deep in thought. "It's obviously his calling card, but why?"

The guys threw out possibilities and discussed the merits of each idea.

He glanced at Cassidy, who had been too quiet and hadn't added her opinions in several minutes.

She sat and stared at the Christmas tree, her eyes shifting back and forth.

Kyle wondered what occupied her thoughts. He refrained from disturbing her. He knew how hard it was for ideas to coalesce.

She jerked her head up and snapped her fingers. "The four quarters."

"There were nine, Cassidy." Keith corrected her.

"No. Not the ones we discovered but the ones at John Morrison's office. He has a frame of four quarters. I remember now that when I originally interviewed him, I asked him about the significance of it. Since four friends started the business, they got four quarters with the year they launched the company, symbolizing the first dollar earned."

"You really think Morrison killed his friends?" Keith asked.

"Why not? He's now the sole owner of the company." She tapped her chin. "Either that or someone wants to make him look guilty."

"If he was having business problems, there are easier ways to resolve them than murdering the people involved, though." Doug sighed.

"A setup is an interesting concept." Jason drummed his fingers on the arm of his chair. "Who had it out for Morrison?"

"I haven't found anything to suggest that." Doug retrieved his laptop. "Based on that idea, I'll target my search to include enemies."

Kyle sorted the new ideas in his head. He doodled on the notepad in his lap, half listening to the discussion going on around him. He circled Aaron's name.

"Kyle?" Cassidy rested her hand on his arm. "What is it?"

His coworkers stopped talking and looked at him.

"I'm wondering about Aaron Perkins." He tapped the tip of his pen on the man's name.

Cassidy shifted to face Kyle. "What about him?"

"They never found his body." He glanced up.

Her eyes widened. "You think he faked his death?"

Kyle shrugged. "I'm only throwing out the idea."

"It's possible." Dennis's scowl deepened. "Keith, I want a full workup on the investigation. Talk to every officer, tech and diver that worked that case. I want to know if there's anything that hints at Aaron staging his own death."

"On it, boss." Keith scribbled down notes.

"I want that warrant for Morrison," Cassidy said.

"It's iffy that a judge will agree to it even with the new information." Kyle hated to speak the reality of the situation, but what they had was slim.

Dennis blew out a breath. "I'll try. It's a stretch, but we might get the warrant if I spin it just right."

Kyle could tell Cassidy wanted to argue, but she held on to her composure.

"That's all I ask. It's time to trust the system and send up a few prayers that God will help us solve these cases." Cassidy exhaled.

Jason nodded. "I agree."

"I'll make the call. Y'all start praying." Dennis excused himself and headed to the kitchen for privacy.

One by one, the guys closed their eyes. He noticed Cassidy hesitate, then follow their lead. The room became quiet.

Prayer. Kyle had leaned on his faith for the past year. He'd never have made it without God by his side. Chats with Him on a daily occurrence. But that was the problem. He hadn't had a long conversation with Him in a long time. Maybe the time had come to quit hiding behind his guilt and shame and make God a top priority again.

God, I'm sorry for not treating You like the best friend You are. I'm sorry for the quick words and for not taking the time to really talk with You. But until we can have that conversation, could You please help us get the information we need to put this killer behind bars?

One at a time, his friends opened their eyes and waited to hear about the warrant.

Dennis strode in. "We got it."

"Yes!" Jason and Keith gave each other a high five.

"Kyle, you and Cassidy pick it up when it's ready in the morning. It's for Morrison's office. The judge wouldn't add his home, but I'll take what I can get." Dennis placed his hands on the back of the chair he'd vacated. "Everyone else, keep at your current assignments in case we're off about this guy."

After several more minutes of conversation, the guys said their goodbyes and left.

Alone with Cassidy in the living room, Kyle steeled his nerves. He had to talk to her about the almost kiss.

"Cassidy, about earlier."

"Let's focus on the case for now."

"But—"

She shook her head. "I'm going to see if Doug needs help with dinner." She walked away.

Kyle stood staring at her back.

What had changed in the last couple of hours?

FOURTEEN

The hum of the truck tires raked on Kyle's nerves. After Dennis secured the search warrant and everyone had left last night, Kyle tried to talk to Cassidy about what happened between them, but she'd brushed him off.

Had he misjudged her interest? She seemed a willing participant in their almost kiss. Then again, he understood. Caring beyond friendship for Amber's best friend was just—weird. Plus, the risk of falling in love again had him questioning his thoughts. But he couldn't deny the direction of his heart.

The more his feelings got involved, the more Judith's advice made sense. He and Cassidy shared memories—why not embrace them? But unless she agreed, he wouldn't have a future with her. He had to fix his mistake.

"I overstepped the boundaries last night. I shouldn't have done that." He glanced at her. The tears swimming in her eyes jolted him. Had he messed up that badly? "Cass, I'm sorry."

She blew out a quick breath and shook her head.

His hateful words toward her when he'd accused her of being reckless ran in his mind on repeat. He'd done it again. But hadn't they gotten past the anger before yesterday's meeting?

God, when will I learn? How do I make this better?

Decision made. He had to tell her he was falling in love with her, even if she turned him down.

Cassidy spoke first. "Last night, I should have been honest with you." Her voice quavered. "I—" Her eyes widened, and she screamed.

He turned in time to see a black SUV speeding in their direction, seconds before it smashed into the front side of them. Because of the angle, the airbags didn't deploy.

The truck skidded across the pavement. The rear wheels jumped the curb, and the vehicle jerked to a stop. His head bounced on the side window, sending white streaks across his vision. The force of the seat belt snapped him back against the seat. He groaned at the sudden jolt. He fought the churning bile.

When the world stopped moving, and the contents of his stomach agreed to stay put, he reached over and grasped Cassidy's fingers. "Are you okay?"

"I think—" Her hand ripped from his. "Kyle!"

He blinked away the haze and found himself staring at a masked man pulling Cassidy from the truck. A gun to her head.

"Leave her alone!" Kyle fought the seat belt and managed to undo it. A quick yank released his weapon from the holster. He kicked the driver's side door. It creaked on the hinges and flung open. Glock in hand, he stumbled from the wreckage. His legs wobbled as he skirted the vehicle.

The gunman yanked Cassidy against him and used her as a shield. The attacker lifted his weapon at Kyle.

Before it registered what was happening, the man fired.

Kyle flew backward and hit the ground with a thud. He gasped, but air refused to fill his lungs.

Cassidy cried out to him, but his body wouldn't cooperate. His Kevlar vest had saved his life, but the bruise on his chest from the impact of the bullet burned like being stabbed with a hot poker.

He rolled his head to the side in time to see the shooter shove her into the SUV. A moment later, they drove off.

He forced himself to his hands and knees and staggered to his feet. "Cassidy!"

The taillights of the SUV vanished in the distance.

I'll find you, Cassidy. I promise.

The attacker had slipped plastic cuffs on her wrists, secured her to the SUV and sped off, leaving Kyle lying dead in the middle of the road.

The man beside her had killed Kyle, and she couldn't do anything to save him. A seasoned officer and she'd allowed the man to abduct her and let Kyle die. Her failure flashed before her eyes.

Cassidy's world had imploded—again. She'd lost another person she loved.

Her breath hitched. Loved? Yes, she loved him but had resisted admitting it and risking her heart. Kyle had died, never knowing that she wanted a future with him. So what if he hadn't felt the same. At least he would've known her heart.

She choked back the tears of the missed opportunity. She'd allowed her father to dictate her life. His demand that she focus on being the best at everything she did had robbed her of a future with a husband and children.

Not anymore. Assuming she got out of this alive. The revelation of her decision launched another wave of emotion flooding her system. But if she didn't pull it together and think her way out, she'd die at the hands of the man beside her. Cassidy owed it to Kyle to stop his killer so his death wouldn't be in vain.

Wrists zip-tied to the grab handle on the ceiling of the

SUV, she searched for a means to escape. Snapping the ties was out. Even if she broke the plastic cuffs, she'd never escape in time. The man's gun lay in his lap. And he'd proved that he'd use it.

"Why are you doing this, Mr. Morrison?"

The man laughed. "You think I'm that loser? Oh, Detective. I'm disappointed in you."

A familiarity about the man's laugh had her digging through her memories. Could it be Aaron? Had he faked his death and set in motion multiple killings over the past few years? But she'd never heard Aaron's voice, and she'd heard this guy before. But where?

It clicked into place. She sucked in a breath. She'd been *that* wrong about Morrison? Kyle had tried to make her slow down and not jump to conclusions. Hindsight—a wonderful thing. She saw it now. Her desperation to solve Laura's case had taken over and clouded her judgment. Not the computer mogul, but Aaron's friend, Robert Hansen. How had she missed that?

"Robert Hansen."

"Are you sure about that?" His white teeth glinted through the mouth hole in the mask.

Oh, she was sure all right. She recognized his voice from his voicemail greeting when she'd tried to call. But why had he killed so many people? She let the puzzle pieces float in her mind until they began to fit together. It was all in the timing.

"You killed Laura because she saw you at the scene when you killed Sandy and Michael Hughes. Even though she had no idea what she'd witnessed, because if she had, she'd have told me, you couldn't allow her to identify you."

"It took me a couple of days to find her. But it worked out for the better. It allowed me time to set up her *accident*."

"That's why the coin matched her birth year."

"Give the lady a prize." Hansen turned onto the drive that headed to the marina at the lake. Soon, he pulled to a stop and parked the SUV near the dock. "Stay there." He chuckled and got out of the vehicle.

The SUV door clunked closed like a lid on a coffin. She shivered but forced her mind to focus.

Until now, her brain had refused to remember all the facts before the apartment fire. The whole scene fell into place. He'd killed those in powerful positions. And those that didn't fit his victim type, like her cousin, had been in the wrong place at the wrong time. He'd eliminated anyone who could identify him. Laura had seen him, and it had cost her her life.

And unless God saved her, Cassidy had no hope of getting out of this alive and would join Laura in death at the hands of Robert Hansen.

Cassidy yanked on her bindings. The plastic cut into her wrists, leaving slices in her scars. Blood dripped down her arms inside her sleeve.

She'd failed to see the obvious in front of her due to her arrogance. Her father's demand for excellence and the climb to the top of the proverbial ladder had skewed her view of life and the case. If only she'd taken a step back, put her pride of insisting on doing it herself aside and embraced the help around her, she'd have seen the clues. She felt like an idiot.

The pursuit of perfection had hindered her life choices—work and personal. She loved her dad, but why had she let him dictate her life? Pushing her to be the best at everything. That ambition had left her with a feeling of inadequacy and a hole in her heart. A hole that only one man could satisfy—Kyle Howard. Now she'd live with a giant void that would remain unfilled for the rest of her life.

Cassidy had to survive to bring justice to those she loved. She searched for someone—anyone nearby. The dockmaster. If she screamed loud enough, maybe he'd hear her and call for help.

The car door creaked on its hinges, and the cold December air drifted into the SUV, making her shiver.

She willed her pulse to slow. It was now or never. If he got her on a boat…

Before she had the opportunity to scream, Robert slapped duct tape over her mouth. He clipped the ties loose from the handle and jerked her out of the car.

She staggered and tipped forward, landing on her knee. Her jeans tore, and blood stained the denim.

Robert yanked her upright, pulled her tight against him and shoved the gun into her side. "Walk." He aimed them toward the dock in the opposite direction of the dockmaster.

Tears burned her eyes. She'd climbed the law enforcement ranks. And for what? More responsibility. She wanted more in life than reaching for the top. She wanted Kyle.

If the slimmest chance existed that he'd lived, she wanted a future with him.

Cassidy had to escape.

Kyle staggered to his truck. The breath he pulled in sent daggers through his chest. He wiped at the blood oozing from a gash on the side of his head where he'd hit the window. He'd survived the crash and the gunshot, but his heart had taken a direct hit when the masked man fled with Cassidy in his clutches.

The bruise from the bullet's impact spread under his Kevlar vest. His numb fingers fumbled with the Velcro straps. The pieces ripped apart, and he slid his hand under the heavy material. The relief was immediate. The contact site continued to throb, but the pressure had disappeared.

He leaned against the wrecked truck for support and dug his cell phone from his pocket. Face tilted toward the sky, Kyle hit speed dial.

"Olsen."

"Doug, he has her." Kyle had waited too long to admit his feelings, another regret to add to the list.

"Hang on, partner. I'm on my way."

"She's gone, man." He swiped a hand down his face. Blood streaked his palm.

"We'll find her." Kyle almost believed Doug's determined words.

Sirens wailed.

Kyle pressed a steadying hand on the hood of the truck. Steam vented from the crumpled metal, a reminder of his failure to keep her safe. He had to find Cassidy—had to save her. Had to tell her he loved her.

If he were honest, he'd never been angry at her. She'd been easy to blame, and he'd taken a swipe at her law enforcement abilities. The disappointment in his action had him dropping his chin to his chest.

Tires squealed, and boots pounded on the pavement.

He lifted his gaze.

Doug jogged toward him. "Do you need an ambulance?"

"No. My injuries can wait. We have to find Cassidy before that man kills her."

Valley Springs PD arrived along with the fire department. The chaos around them increased. The sounds and lights made his skin crawl and his head pound. He took a step and swayed.

Doug gripped Kyle's arm and guided him to his SUV. "We found evidence of someone blackmailing Morrison. He paid hefty amounts to stay alive, afraid to go to the police, seeing so many he knew knocked off one by one. Plus, his alibis check out. He couldn't have committed most of the crimes or the attacks on Cassidy. He's cleared."

"Then who is it?" Kyle rubbed his forehead. When his fingers touched the new gash, he winced.

"Jason and Keith are poring over the documents as we speak to see who he paid."

Kyle climbed into the passenger side of the vehicle and rested against the headrest.

His partner slid behind the wheel and turned up the heat. "Any idea where the killer took her?"

Flipping through the imaginary files in his mind, he searched for a clue—any clue to where the guy had taken Cassidy. Kyle jolted forward. He scrambled for his phone.

"What is it?" Doug shifted to look at him.

"I gave her a necklace with a GPS tracker in it." He clicked the series of icons.

"Does she know you did that?"

Kyle nodded. "Of course. She didn't like the idea, but she agreed to it." He stared at the app, waiting for it to load her location. "Got it. Head to the marina."

"I don't like the sounds of that."

"Me either." Kyle snapped on his seat belt and searched for the dockmaster's number.

"I'll tell PD you'll give your statement later." Doug jumped out, filled in the officers, then raced back to the SUV. He radioed in the details and hit the accelerator.

Kyle clicked on the phone number. "Come on. Hurry up and answer."

"Myers Lake Marina. Dockmaster Eddie Jones speaking."

"Eddie, this is Kyle Howard."

"Hey, Kyle, how's it going?"

"Not good." Eddie was a decent guy and friend, but

Kyle didn't have time for small talk. "Did a man and woman come down there?"

"I've been doing paperwork, but I did see a couple head to a boat." A chair squeaked. "In fact, they're taking the boat out now."

Kyle's stomach dropped to his toes. "Can you stop them?"

"Sorry, they're already leaving the marina."

"Keep an eye on that boat." Kyle hung up. "We have to hurry. If he gets her on the lake…" The words died on his lips.

"I know." Doug's cell rang, and he punched the speaker button. "Olsen."

"How's Kyle?" Jason's demanding tone startled him.

He shook off the fog surrounding him. "I'm right here. Took a bullet to the vest, but I'll live. It's Cassidy that I'm not so sure about. The killer took her."

Doug whipped around a corner. The SUV skidded, then caught traction.

Kyle's seat belt locked, snapping him back against the seat. He groaned at the pressure on his growing bruise.

"Sorry." Doug sped up. "What do you have for us, Jason?"

"We know it's not Morrison. But we haven't narrowed it down yet."

"Give us anything you have." Kyle braced his hand on the dash. "Anything at all."

"I'm looking at the interviews you asked me to review. The vice president of Morrison's company, Robert Hansen, went to college with the original four, not just Aaron."

"I knew he and Aaron had a friendship, but he knew the others in college as well?"

"Yes. Keith talked with Hansen's wife. The group was tight during school. When the four started their business and left Robert out of the plan, he went into a deep depression. The wife said it took a while, but he pulled it together and got a great job. Then his boss cheated him out of a huge commission and ultimately fired him. That happened two years ago, about the time the first set of killings that Cassidy tagged happened," Jason said.

"Assuming there's a serial killer and he's the suspect, that's what triggered him." Kyle adjusted the shoulder harness away from his chest.

"Sounds like it."

"So, what? He asked John Morrison to hire him?" Doug asked.

Paper rustled on Jason's end. "From what we can tell, Morrison did that under duress. We're working on proving the blackmailer was Hansen."

How had Kyle gotten it so wrong?

"The sheriff has a search warrant and is at Hansen's house now with VSPD," Jason said.

"If you're right about all this, then it has to be Robert who has Cassidy, and he's headed out of the marina by boat. We're several minutes behind them, but Doug is breaking all kinds of speed limits." For which Kyle was thankful. "We might need backup, pending what we find."

"Keith and I are on the way." Jason hung up.

Kyle tipped his head back against the seat. "I did it again."

"Are you talking about that ridiculous idea that your last words will cause her harm?" Doug sighed. "Look, now is not the time to have this discussion, but mark my words, we will have it. But the bottom line is, you are not responsible for the things that happen out of your control."

He swiped a hand down his face. "Yeah, I got that. I still feel horrible, though."

"If anyone understands, it's me." Doug's hand tightened on the steering wheel. "Just promise me you won't leave things hanging with Cassidy when we get her back."

"*If* we get her back." Kyle held up a hand and stopped his partner's objection. "But…that's a promise I can keep."

"Good." Doug raced into the parking lot and parked next to Robert's car.

Kyle slid his 9 mm Glock from his holster. "I've got the car. Cover me." He and Doug jumped from the vehicle. Kyle's legs buckled, but he caught himself and held his gun at ready. Four strides and he stood aiming his weapon at the driver's side window. "No one is in there."

"Hey!" The dockmaster waved his arms. "They're out there." He pointed at the water.

A boat raced away from the marina and bounced on the waves as they sped across the lake.

Kyle squinted. Two figures appeared as dots on the fast-moving vessel. "Doug, call for backup!" Kyle raced to the sheriff's department boat in a slip near the boathouse.

The cold air swirled around him. The temperature continued to drop. Not a night anyone would want to be stuck outside without shelter.

He snatched the keys from the lockbox, released the ropes, then sprang onto the boat. The engine turned over, and he pressed the throttle forward. The boat sped from the marina.

The water sprayed over the edges of the boat, leaving freezing droplets on his cheeks. He ignored the discomfort from his hands, cold from the wetness and the open air, and focused on reaching Cassidy before the worst happened.

If Robert decided to throw her overboard, she'd never last more than a couple of minutes in the frigid lake.

His stomach roiled at the thought. He loved her. He couldn't lose her too.

God, don't let me be late.

* * *

The boat engine whined, drowning out all other sounds. Cassidy sat in the back, hands bound in front of her. Her cheeks hurt where Robert had ripped off the duct tape from her mouth once they had moved out of ear shot of the dockmaster. She struggled against the nausea the rough waters and motion of the boat caused.

Why had she waited to tell Kyle that she loved him? Her chest hurt, knowing she'd never say those words to him. She understood the old saying "dying from a broken heart." But she couldn't dwell on that now. She had a killer to stop because if she didn't, he'd get away with multiple murders, including Kyle's.

With an awkward grip, she used the bench to hoist herself to her feet. She staggered toward Robert but lost her balance and fell. Her side hit a metal bar, and she cried out. Damp strands of hair blew across her face, sticking to her cheeks and eyelashes. Cassidy raised her arm and wiped the offending pieces away.

Robert turned. A wicked grin spread across his face. "Problem, Detective?" He chuckled and continued to aim the boat farther out into the middle of the lake. "You're the best prize yet. Detectives…they think they're so smart." His laugh echoed on the water. "And that cousin of yours just had to be nosey. I didn't have time to do my research. I like to watch and toy with my victims. But she saw me shoot Sandy and Michael. I had to eliminate her. Who would have thought you had a pact not to drink? If I'd known, I wouldn't have used vaporized alcohol."

Anger bubbled inside. He'd killed Laura and smirked about it. Cassidy pushed to her feet and charged at him, taking him by surprise. She latched on to his wrist and slammed it on the wheel. The gun he'd kept in his hand skittered across the deck.

He regained his balance and backhanded her across the face.

Her head whipped back. She reached out to brace herself. The plastic cuffs bit into her skin, and she tumbled to the deck.

"Too bad no one will find your body. At least I don't have to be careful about bruises." The evil smile returned to his face.

He eased back on the throttle. The boat slowed and bobbed in the waves, adding to her swirling belly.

The icy breeze cut into her damp clothes, and blood trickled from the cuts on her cheek and wrists. Her energy waned, but she refused to give up without a fight. Cassidy clutched the necklace Kyle had given her.

God, if Kyle's gone, please let Doug know about the GPS.

With renewed determination, she stumbled to a standing position, ready for round two.

A boat engine hummed in the distance. Hope sprang inside, and she glanced over her shoulder. A critical mistake.

Robert grabbed her legs. "In you go." He yanked her feet up. Her head crashed into the side rail, and she fell into the icy December water with a splash.

The freezing water stole her breath. She sucked in a mouthful before going under. With a quick surge to the surface, she coughed to clear her lungs.

Her boots and coat, soaked with water, pulled her under. She fought to stay above the water, but the zip ties made it impossible to free herself of the bulky clothes.

Tears filled her eyes. She was going to die, and Hansen would get away with another murder.

She'd failed Laura and now Kyle.

I'm so sorry that I didn't get justice for you.

If she had it to do again, she'd live a joy-filled life, not one focused on being the best at everything. Because look where that got her. Dying in the middle of a lake alone.

The light from above dimmed as the water engulfed her and dragged her down. Her lungs burned, begging for oxygen. Darkness closed around her.

The last thought that flitted through her mind was of Kyle.

What if he was alive?

The scream that pierced the air moments ago when Cassidy had gone overboard sent a dagger through Kyle's heart. He'd found her too late to save her from the freezing water.

"Cassidy!" He scanned the lake, praying she surfaced. He hadn't heard a gunshot, but who knew what had happened between the noises of the boat engines and the wind.

He had to stop Hansen and save Cassidy.

Kyle pulled his craft next to Robert's boat and jumped on. He tackled the man, sending him sprawling on the deck. The impact on his bruised chest sent waves of pain through his torso. He gasped but forced himself to stand.

Robert grabbed the fire extinguisher and swung.

Kyle wasn't quick enough to dodge the metal canister, and it made contact with his thigh. He lost traction and stumbled.

Robert dashed for the throttle. The engine revved, and the boat jumped forward.

He'd run out of time to stop Hansen. He had a choice, and he'd choose Cassidy every time. Kyle jumped into the water. Cassidy's life depended on it.

The boat sped off.

Kyle hoped his fellow law enforcement officers caught

Robert, but he'd worry about that later. Cassidy needed him. He had to find her and get her to shore before she drowned or hypothermia took her life.

For a brief moment, she appeared. She coughed and sputtered.

A small wave peaked, engulfing her.

Heart in his throat, he swam to the spot where she'd gone below the surface. He dived down, searching by feel, and came up empty. His heart rate skyrocketed. He had to find her. She couldn't die on him.

Determined not to stop, he treaded water and scanned the area, looking for any sign of where she might be. The cold water stole his energy and made his limbs sluggish. Cassidy only had a few minutes left. He had to hurry, for both of their sakes.

After one more check, confirming she hadn't resurfaced, Kyle sucked in a breath. If he didn't find her this time, he might not have the ability to make another attempt. He dipped below the water, hand out, praying he'd touch her.

God, help me find her.

His fingers tangled with strands of hair. Relief hit him so hard he wanted to sob.

He grabbed a handful and pulled. They broke the surface. An arm wrapped under her, and he swam to the sheriff's department boat that had drifted and now bobbed in the water. He pushed her onto the ramp and hefted himself aboard with what little strength he had left.

His teeth chattered, and he struggled to catch his breath. The icy water clung to him, making it difficult to move.

The color of Cassidy's skin sent his stomach to his toes.

"Wake up, Cassidy. Please." He shook her shoulder, but she didn't respond. He'd been too late.

Hand under her nose, he waited for a breath to brush

against his fingers, but none came. He leaned down, covered her mouth with his, and gave two breaths. "Come on, Cass. Don't leave me." When she didn't move, he gave her two more breaths.

She coughed and sputtered. Water bubbled in her mouth.

Kyle rolled her on her side, and the liquid poured from her lips. "That's it, Cass. Get it out." Once he felt it safe, he lifted her against his chest.

Half sitting, half lying, and wrists still cuffed, she curled her arms around his. Coughs racked her body until a full breath entered her lungs. "Kyle? Thought…dead." Tears flooded her eyes.

"I'm here, honey."

"Robert. He…"

"I know, Cass. I know. You can tell me about it later." He rubbed her back.

Her teeth chattered, and her body shook. "So cold."

"I'm sorry I was late."

"'S okay." The slur in Cassidy's words worried him. He had to get her to the hospital.

"Let's get the flex-cuffs off you, and I'll find a blanket." He removed his pocket knife and snapped the plastic.

Shivering, she hugged her body. "He got away."

"Don't worry about it. The guys will find him. Come on. Let's get you moved under the canopy."

Hand under her elbow, he helped her stand. She wobbled, and her knees buckled. Kyle scooped her into his arms and carried her to the sheltered area of the boat.

Once protected from the bulk of the wind, he laid her on the bench seat. "I'll be right back." He rushed to the chest of supplies and pulled out two wool blankets. If he didn't get warm soon, he'd succumb to the cold as well, and that wouldn't help Cassidy.

"Here you go." He snuggled her in the blanket, then

wrapped the other around himself. One last look at her, and his pulse raced. Her blue lips were the least of his worries. The translucent look of her skin scared him to death. Hypothermia and time had collided. He had to hurry.

Kyle cranked the engine and pushed the throttle forward. Turning the wheel, he aimed the boat toward the marina and grabbed the radio. "Dockmaster, this is Sheriff One."

"Copy that, Kyle. Go ahead."

"I need an ambulance and a BOLO on Robert Hansen."

"BOLO is out. And the ambulance is here waiting by the dock. Your partner already called it in."

Bless the man. "Copy that."

"Kyle, this is Doug. What's the medical emergency?"

He wanted to laugh. More than likely, Doug had commandeered the radio without asking. "Cassidy and I took a dip in the lake. She's hypothermic and inhaled a lot of water. I had to do mouth-to-mouth. She's breathing, but her skin…" The words got stuck in his throat.

"Understood. I'll relay the info to Rachel and Peter."

"Thanks."

"How about you?" Doug asked.

"Freezing. I need a cup of hot coffee, or three, and a warm shower, but I'll survive."

"I hear what you're not saying."

Yeah, his partner read him like no other on most days. An annoying little habit of Doug's.

"We'll see you in a couple of minutes." The dockmaster had taken back the radio.

"Copy that. Be there as soon as I can." A few minutes later, Kyle maneuvered the boat to the dock and shut off the engine.

Doug jumped on board and tossed the rope to the dockmaster, who tied off the boat.

Kyle lifted Cassidy into his arms.

She moaned, but her eyes remained closed.

"I've got you, Cass. You'll be warm soon." He tucked her next to his chest and stepped onto the dock, praying his legs didn't give out.

The paramedics met him at the end of the wooden planks.

Peter maneuvered the gurney around. "Here." He helped Kyle secure Cassidy. "You look like you can use medical too."

"Focus on her. I'll be fine." He'd require a change of clothes sooner versus later, but he wanted all the attention on Cassidy.

Rachel shook her head and rolled her eyes. "Right." She assisted Peter in rolling the gurney to the ambulance and sliding it into the back. Rachel climbed in. Her hands moved at a rapid rate connecting monitors and inserting an IV.

Peter closed the doors and placed a hand on Kyle's shoulder. "We'll take good care of her." The paramedic jutted his chin at him. "Get dry before you end up in the ambulance beside her."

Kyle stood stock still as the medic unit pulled from the parking lot, taking the woman he was falling in love with.

"She's in good hands." Doug draped the blanket that Kyle had dropped over his shoulders. "And don't forget, she's a fighter. That'll help."

"What if I didn't get to her in time, and she has permanent damage from her near drowning?" He tugged the blanket tighter. The weight of depression pressed down on him. What if he lost her too?

Doug placed a hand on Kyle's back. "Who's in control?"

"God." He knew the answer, but what if he didn't like the outcome?

FIFTEEN

When Kyle rescued Cassidy from the icy grave and drove her to the dock, she'd lain on the bench. Her teeth had chattered to the point she thought they might crack, and her skin burned from the frigid water.

Funny how cold and hot had a similar effect if extreme enough.

The ambulance bumped on the road, sending a zing of pain through her. She whimpered.

"Cassidy?"

She opened her eyes and squinted at Rachel.

"There you are." The paramedic adjusted the IV and lifted Cassidy's wrist. "I'll clean these up and see what the damage is."

Too tired to speak, Cassidy met the woman's gaze and nodded.

"You know, the guys always demand lollipops." Rachel wetted gauze and wiped at the cuts left by the flex-cuffs. "It's become a running joke, but I think they're just little boys at heart. They certainly act like it at times. And make the worst patients." The paramedic lowered Cassidy's arm and lifted the other.

Rachel's soft tones lulled Cassidy into a sense of safety and calm. Before she knew it, the woman had completed her task. "You did that on purpose?" Cassidy's voice came out as a whisper.

"Guilty. It's easier if you aren't focused on what I'm doing." The paramedic grinned. "Most people don't catch on to my methods." Rachel added another blanket. "You're doing fine. Go ahead and relax. They'll stabilize your temperature at the hospital, and you'll be up and going in no time."

Cassidy wanted to respond—she really did—but the cold had zapped her energy. She closed her eyes and let herself drift to sleep.

Once at the hospital, the heated blankets weighed down on her sensitive skin, and the doctors ran warmed saline through her IV. Not exactly painful, but close. Grateful for the assist in raising her core temperature, she'd endured the odd sensation. But would be glad when it was finally over.

When she'd arrived, the doctor told her that Kyle had saved her life by doing mouth-to-mouth resuscitation. She had no recollection of his efforts. Probably a good thing. The idea of swimming even in warm water made her heart skip a beat.

Several hours later, in her private room, Cassidy tugged the blanket closer to her chin. The doctor had admitted her overnight for observation. She'd balked at the idea but, in the end, had given up and complied.

She lifted a coffee mug from the roller table and took a sip. The nurse had stopped the heated saline that helped maintain her core temperature a while back and had brought her hot beverages instead. The warm liquids helped, but she'd had enough that if she got up and walked around, she'd slosh.

"Knock, knock." Kyle peeked in. "May I come in?"

She motioned for him to join her. "You look better than when I last saw you."

"Back at ya. But yeah, a hot shower and dry clothes will do that." He sat in the easy chair near her bed and scooted closer. "Did the sheriff come and take your statement."

"About thirty minutes ago." She ran her finger along the rim of her cup. "Did they catch Robert?"

Kyle smiled. "He's in custody as we speak."

"Is he talking?"

"Oh yeah. Once the sheriff explained they found his stash of trophies from his victims, Robert told his attorney to leave and confessed to all the crimes you indicated and a few more. Being left out of his friends' start-up company and then tossed out of the company he'd worked for triggered his rage and his need to eliminate people in power positions. After he failed to kill Morrison in the hit-and-run, he blackmailed the man to keep him silent. Morrison never went to the police because he was afraid Hansen would somehow implicate him or finish his attempt to kill him off. And since Hansen is something of a tech expert, he was able to hide the 4Gen Tech business partners from the search engines to hide his connection to the victims.

"Seems the man is rather proud of himself. Between our statements from today, his confession of the murders and blackmailing Morrison, plus the evidence collected from his home, Robert Hansen is going away for a very long time."

"You mean I'm finally safe?" Cassidy asked.

Kyle reached over and brushed a strand of hair from her forehead. "Yes."

She swiped at the single tear trickling down her cheek. "I thought I'd be relieved. Satisfied maybe, once I knew the truth about Laura. But I feel hollow inside." More like an abyss in her chest. Her cousin had held her hand during her hospital stay while Cassidy recovered from her burns and the loss of Amber. She missed them both so much.

He reached between the bed rails and laced his fingers with hers. "It's hard. You think the truth will fix your broken heart, but it doesn't. Only time will soothe the pain, but I don't think it ever goes away."

She had forgotten Kyle had suffered the loss of his parents and previous partner, and more recently, his fiancée. "I'm sorry you had to go through all that."

He shrugged. "I'm glad I had God to lean on. If not, I'd be a mess." Kyle ran his fingers through his hair and chuckled. "Okay, more of a mess."

She squeezed his hand. "I should have let myself remember, but I held back. And because of that, it all came crashing down."

"I may have overreacted."

"Really?" Cassidy tilted her head and smirked.

"Brat." He hadn't teased her in so long, it felt like an old friend coming home.

Did she dare speak the truth? If her experience had taught her anything, it was to take a risk with her heart and let God take care of the rest. "Kyle, I..."

"Before you say anything. I have a confession." He closed his eyes. The creases in his forehead deepened.

When he opened them, Cassidy struggled to breathe. The warmth of his gaze set her heart racing. Could he feel the same as she did?

"I blamed you for Amber's death from the beginning. It was easier than facing my own guilt. I was wrong. I should have been there for you." Kyle rubbed the back of his neck with his free hand. "Cassidy, I... I'm falling in love with you. Part of me feels guilty. It's only been nine months since Amber died. But I can't deny what's in here." He tapped his chest.

Cassidy swallowed the lump building in her throat.

She, too, felt something more sparking between them and understood the guilt.

"We had a great friendship before, and now that some maniac isn't after you, I'm curious if you're interested in more." His knee bounced at a rapid rate.

"Kyle."

He pulled his hand away, but she tugged him back. Poor guy thought she planned to turn him down. She'd better get the words out before he got the wrong idea.

"Let me finish." She smiled at him, attempting to relieve his worry. "I think more would be wonderful. I've liked you for a long time—as a friend. But when trouble came our way, I saw deep into your heart. I knew I wanted to be with you. Only I hesitated because of Amber."

"We both are adjusting to a world without her. But as Judith practically knocked me over the head with, it's okay to keep Amber close in our hearts. Share the memories. And move on together." He blew out a breath. His shoulders relaxed. "What do you say we start with today and see what tomorrow brings."

Cassidy knew Amber would want them both to be happy. That's the kind of friend she was. "Judith is a wise woman. I'd like that very much."

He stood and leaned over the bed rail, his brown eyes searching, asking for permission.

She nodded and closed the distance.

His lips touched hers in the sweetest kiss of promise she'd ever experienced.

Her heart exploded with hope of a future with him.

A crisp cool Christmas morning breeze, the perfect backdrop for visiting Amber's grave.

Kyle and Cassidy had joined his friends at the Christmas Eve service the night before. He'd felt more at peace than he had in a long time.

He held a wreath in one hand and clutched Cassidy's hand with the other. He had a hard time believing she wanted to explore a future with him after his jerk attitude toward her when Amber died.

His heart had taken the first steps to healing, and Cassidy played a big part in that.

As they approached Amber's gravesite, his stomach tightened. "Is it me, or is this awkward?"

Cassidy chuckled. "Maybe a bit."

"Phew, glad it's not just me." He joined her laughter.

Silence grew between them as they stepped closer to the grave.

The dried leaves crunched beneath his boots. The air smelled of coming snow. A sad smile tugged at his lips.

After his parents had died on Christmas Eve, he'd struggled through the season. He'd avoided decorating and refused to attend Christmas Eve church services for the first few years. Not that he'd walked away from God. More like he hadn't wanted to endure the reminder of what he'd lost. It was hard to celebrate his Savior and grieve his parents at the same time.

Eventually, the pain faded. When he'd met Amber, she and Cassidy had taken it upon themselves to create happy memories. And that they had. An amazing friendship had connected the three of them.

He squeezed Cassidy's hand. Over the past few days, she'd helped him experience a renewed love for Christmas and the hope the day symbolized. Now, she stood beside him, giving him her strength. He'd like to think he did the same for her.

The gray granite headstone rose above the ground like a

beacon. Etched in the stone: "Amber Sue Lofton. Precious daughter, fiancée and friend."

Emotion clogged his throat. He'd visited before, but today was different. Thanks to the woman next to him, his heart had started to heal.

Kyle came not to say goodbye but to let go of the past.

Cassidy released his hand and placed a potted poinsettia next to the grave. "She loved you, Kyle. So much she'd planned to talk you into getting married on Christmas Day."

A squeak escaped his lips. "Christmas Day?"

"Yes. She wanted to replace the pain of your parents' death with your wedding day, but she hesitated. I convinced her it was the perfect plan."

When had she decided that? "Amber never said anything."

"Because she died that day."

"Oh, Cassidy." He might have been engaged to Amber, but Cassidy had found a way to speak to his heart. "Thank you. It means a lot even though it didn't happen."

He knelt on the damp ground, picked a few twigs from the front of the grave and tossed them aside. With trembling hands, he placed the Christmas wreath against the headstone and stood. "It was her favorite time of year."

"It's perfect." Cassidy slipped her arm around his waist and tugged him close.

Kyle rested his cheek on the top of her head. "Do you think she's okay that we're together?" He felt her body shake. Was she laughing or crying? He pulled away and turned her to face him. "Cassidy?"

She shook her head. "You'll never believe me."

He tucked a flyaway strand behind her ear. "Tell me."

"One night, when we were being particularly morbid after a tough case, she said that if anything happened to her, she wanted both of us to be happy." She shrugged. "And what better way than together." Cassidy pinched her lips, but her shoulders shook.

"What's so funny about that?"

"Other than she followed it up with a teasing 'until then, you can't have him. He's mine.' Of course, I had no intention of even thinking in that direction. We were friends, but only friends." She faked a shudder and peered up at him. "It would have been like kissing my brother. No thank you."

He rolled his eyes, but laughter bubbled inside. Yeah, he agreed. He'd only had eyes for Amber. But that was then. "And now?"

She rose on her tiptoes and brushed a kiss on his lips. "I think I'll stick around to see what happens."

"Good." He wrapped his arms around her and held her tight.

When he let go, he stepped closer to Amber's grave and placed a hand on the cold stone. *I loved you from the first time I saw you, Amber. You'll always have a place in my heart, but it's time to let you go and move on with my life.* He glanced back at Cassidy and back to the headstone. *I'll take good care of her.*

Cassidy tilted her head. "Ready?"

"More than." He moved next to her and took her hand. His heart, lighter than it had been in nine months. It would take time, but the future with Cassidy lay like a golden path in front of him.

His phone buzzed in his pocket. He checked the text message and smiled.

Cassidy bumped him. "Are you going to share?"

"It's Jason. Melanie's in labor."

Cassidy squealed. "A Christmas baby."

"Want to go stalk the hospital hallways?"

"Yes, please." She smiled.

Even though they had hours to wait, he and Cassidy hurried to the new truck he'd purchased two days ago.

Only God would construct such a turning point for him on Christmas Day. Peace about the past, a job he loved with great friends and a new opportunity with the woman next to him. And he couldn't forget the new life ready to make an appearance in the world.

God, thank You seems so inadequate. But thank You from the bottom of my heart.

EPILOGUE

New Year's Eve

The Christmas lights twinkled on the tree branches in the dimly lit room. Cassidy sat on the couch with Melanie and Jason's new baby girl snuggled in her arms. Her heart exploded with happiness. Life couldn't get much better than this.

The living room remained quiet, but raucous laughter and shenanigans happened not far away in the kitchen and family room at the back of the house.

Kyle leaned in and brushed a hand over the top of the baby's head. "She's beautiful."

Cassidy ran the back of her fingers down the newborn's cheek. The softness turned her insides to jelly. Maybe someday she'd have one of her own. Cassidy released a contented sigh. "I love her name."

"Me too. Noelle is perfect."

"She's our own little Christmas and all the hope that comes with it." Kyle stretched his arm across the back of the couch.

A week had passed, and Cassidy spent every day with Kyle. Their relationship had grown in the short time, but they both agreed to take it slow. She knew he needed time and was willing to give it to him.

"This is quite the date."

He chuckled. "I promised you a wild New Year's Eve five-year-old style."

"That you did. Dennis and Charlotte's girls are a riot. And the dogs… I don't know how they do it."

"With a lot of patience and love." Dennis's soft voice came from behind.

Cassidy leaned her head back and watched him move to the recliner. "Dennis, you are the most chill man I've ever met."

Kyle snorted.

Dennis pinned him with a playful glare. "Keep it to yourself, Howard."

She loved being around this group of friends.

"Are you ever going to share?" Dennis gestured to Noelle.

"Maybe." She smiled but didn't move to hand off the baby.

"That's what I thought." Dennis raised an eyebrow asking her a silent question.

She shook her head.

Kyle's gaze drifted between them. "What are you two up to?"

Excitement flowed through her, yet she hesitated. With their relationship so new, how would he react to her news? Dennis assured her that everything would be fine. But would it?

Cassidy inhaled. She could do this. "Remember when you asked me what I'd do if I had a choice?"

Kyle nodded. "I know you're tired of following your dad's demands and climbing the ranks. But you've never spoken of what you really wanted."

She jutted her chin toward Dennis. "That man over there forced me to take a hard look at my future. Honestly

I think he was worried about you and wanted to know my intentions, but I'll let him off the hook for that."

Dennis chuckled. "You're rather perceptive, Detective. But I do care about you too. You're one of us now."

"You can say that again." She rolled her eyes. If she didn't get on with it, the sheriff would blow her announcement before she could spit it out.

Kyle shifted to look at her. "You two *are* keeping secrets, aren't you?"

She nodded. Might as well get on with it. "I met with Charlotte. And by the way, it must be nice having a resident marriage and family therapist in the group. Anyway, we talked. I realized my father's wishes dictated most of my life choices." More like demands. God had more work to do to help her move beyond the bitterness she'd suppressed. But she'd made progress. "The only thing I stood up for was a career in law enforcement instead of the military. I appreciate all those who choose to serve their country, but I knew it wasn't for me. That said, Charlotte and I discussed my options."

"What did you decide?" No worry laced Kyle's words. Only sincere interest rang from his question.

Noelle squirmed, and Cassidy gently jiggled the baby in her arms until she settled.

Cassidy's gaze met Kyle's. "I want to be a detective, but I also want something a little calmer than drug raids and high-stress SWAT-type situations on a daily basis."

"That sounds reasonable. ACSD has had a few crazy cases lately, but our day-to-day isn't as stressful as yours."

"That's what he said." She gestured to Dennis. "After your sheriff accidently overheard Charlotte and my conversation, he and I talked." Here went nothing. *God, if I'm wrong about this, stop me now.* "He offered me a job with the Anderson County Sheriff's Department."

Kyle's jaw dropped. "But how will…? Can we…us…? This is what you want?"

She lifted baby Noelle to her shoulder and shifted to place her hand on Kyle's arm. "Relax, Kyle. We're good. We can still date. I made sure of that. And yes, this is what I want. I'll be working in the cold case unit."

His brows pinched together. "We don't have a cold case unit."

"We do now." Dennis leaned forward and rested his elbows on his knees. "You guys pull files and work on them when you can, but can't give your undivided attention to them. After a few of our recent cases, I decided to create the position. With Cassidy's experience and tenacity, she'll be a great addition to the department. And you two can continue dating without worry. Not that I would have stopped you, but this is less complicated."

The stunned expression on Kyle's face worried her. Should she have consulted him before taking the job? No. This was what she wanted, no matter what happened between them. For the first time in her life, she looked forward to her future. She prayed it included him.

"Kyle, say something." Cassidy squeezed his arm.

His lips covered hers in a move so quick it surprised her. But only for a second. She slid her free hand behind his head and deepened the kiss.

Dennis cleared his throat.

She pulled away. Her fingers touching her freshly kissed lips, heat crept up her neck and into her cheeks. "Oops."

"Don't worry. He's just jealous it wasn't him and Charlotte." Kyle smiled.

Her new boss chuckled. "True. Now, if you'll excuse me, it's almost midnight, and I want to kiss my wife." Dennis ambled off to find Charlotte.

"I take it you're okay with me working at ACSD."

"More than. I'm happy you're making decisions based on what you want."

"It's rather freeing."

The New Year countdown could be heard from the back of the house.

"Are you ready for the new year?" She met his gaze.

Kyle brushed the back of his hand down her cheek. "As long as it includes you."

"Three…two…one!" Laughter and noise makers filtered in from the other room.

Kyle pulled her into a kiss she'd never forget for the rest of her life.

A kiss of hope and new beginnings.

* * * * *

*If you enjoyed this story by Sami A. Abrams,
pick up the previous books in her
Deputies of Anderson County miniseries:*

Buried Cold Case Secrets
Twin Murder Mix-up
Detecting Secrets

Available now from Love Inspired Suspense!

Dear Reader,

Thank you for reading Kyle and Cassidy's story.

When it comes to holidays, many people struggle with the loss of a loved one, especially around Christmas. Kyle's loss and guilt, along with Cassidy's painful memories, make Christmas a challenge for them.

Christmas, and the hope that comes with it, is a wonderful time of year. But it can be hard to find joy during the season when tragedy and sorrow strike. Like Kyle and Cassidy discovered, the mixture of feelings is difficult to navigate. Their struggle is not unlike our own at times. A good dose of love and understanding go a long way in the healing process.

I'd like to send a special shout-out to my agent, Tamela Hancock Murray, and to my editor, Shana Asaro. You two are the best! I absolutely love working with you. And thank you to my Suspense Squad girls. Knowing there's a group of writers who I can call at any time for writing help or just to laugh is amazing. Thank you, ladies. You're awesome!

I hope you enjoyed reading Kyle and Cassidy's story as much as I did writing it. I'd love to hear from you. You can contact me through my website at samiaabrams.com, where you can also sign up for my newsletter to receive exclusive subscriber giveaways.

Hugs,
Sami A. Abrams